NEWTON RIGG COLLEGE PENRITH

This book is due for return on or before the last date shown below

D1347874

To renew please telephone (01768) 893503 with your library card number.

Part of Askham Bryan College

DAVID BADDIEL

Illustrated by Jim Field

HarperCollins *Children's Books*

First published in hardback in Great Britain by HarperCollins *Children's Books* 2016
HarperCollins *Children's Books* is a division of HarperCollins*Publishers* Ltd
1 London Bridge Street
London SE1 9GF

The HarperCollins *Children's Books* website address is
www.harpercollins.co.uk

1

Text copyright © David Baddiel 2016
Illustrations copyright © Jim Field 2016

David Baddiel and Jim Field assert the moral right
to be identified as the author and illustrator of the work

Hardback ISBN: 978-0-00-818514-5
Trade paperback ISBN: 978-0-00-818515-2

Printed and bound in the UK by
Clays Ltd, St Ives Plc

MIX
Paper from
responsible sources

FSC www.fsc.org   **FSC™ C007454**

FSC™ is a non-profit international organisation established to promote
the responsible management of the world's forests. Products carrying the
FSC label are independently certified to assure consumers that they come
from forests that are managed to meet the social, economic and
ecological needs of present and future generations,
and other controlled sources.

Find out more about HarperCollins and the environment at
www.harpercollins.co.uk/green

To Pip, Tiger, Monkey, Ron
and Chairman Meow

CHAPTER ONE

Enormous furry ears

"Happy birthday to you,

Happy birthday to you,

Happy birthday dear... Maaaallllllcolm!"

Now, this is normally the moment at which the birthday child – whose name in this case (as you may have worked out) is Malcolm – would blow out the candles on their cake.

But the Baileys – that was his full name, Malcolm

Bailey – had a family tradition, which was that they *also* sang 'Happy Birthday' when giving the children their birthday presents. So this song wasn't being sung at a party, and it was not accompanied by a cake. It was just Malcolm's mum and dad (Jackie and Stewart), his grandpa (Theo), his teenage sister (Libby) and his little brother (Bert), on the morning of his eleventh birthday, standing in a circle, in the living room, round a box, covered in wrapping paper (which actually did have printed candles on it).

Malcolm waited for the singing to finish. It was a bit of an annoying tradition, to be honest, because what he *wanted* to do was tear open that wrapping paper. Because he knew that inside the box was what he really, really wanted: a laptop computer.

He had given his parents the exact specification. An FZY Apache 321. Hi-Def screen. 4.0 GHz processor speed. Quad speakers with Nahimic virtual

surround sound. The fastest and coolest and baddest laptop on the planet. He could almost see it in his hands, touch its LED display backlit keyboard.

"...*Happy birthday*

Toooo...

You!"

Smiling at his family, Malcolm reached over to pick up his present.

Finally, he thought.

"For… he's a jolly good fellow!
For he's a jolly good fellow!"

Malcolm leant back, away from the present, still smiling, but through gritted teeth. *Do they normally do this bit?* he thought.

"For he's a jolly good fellow…
And so say all of us!"

"Great! Great singing, guys! Good job! Thanks!" said Malcolm, reaching forward for the present again.

"And… so say all of us!
And so say all of us!

For he's a jolly good fe-eh-llowwww…

And…

So say all of us!!"

His mum and dad and grandpa and sister and brother harmonised – surprisingly well, actually – on the word *us*, making Malcolm think the song must, at last, be over. Not wishing to be disappointed again, he waited five seconds, in case it wasn't. But everyone was just smiling. In fact, his mum was nodding, encouragingly, at the present.

Great, thought Malcolm. And tore open the wrapping.

Oh yes! That computer! With its shiny sleek aluminium cover! And its hyper-sensitive touch pad! And its enormous furry ears!

Malcolm frowned, screwing up his noticeably blue eyes. *Its enormous furry ears…?* He didn't remember reading that specification when he was flicking through photos on BaddestComputer.Net.

But before he could quite work out what was going on, all the others were bending over and putting their faces very, very close to what was being revealed as the wrapping came off.

Which was not, in fact, a computer, or even a cardboard box containing a computer, but… a cage.

"Isn't he the cutest thing?" his mum was saying.

"Look at that sweet face!" his dad was saying.

"OMG! I want to stroke him," his sister was saying.

"I want to eat him!" his little brother was saying.

"He reminds me of Lord Kitchener!" his grandpa was saying.

"Sorry," said Malcolm. "What *is* this?"

"Well, Malc…" said Jackie.

"Mum!"

"Sorry."

"I've *told* you, Mum."

Malcolm didn't like being called Malc. He wasn't

sure why. Possibly because it rhymed with talc, and thus made him think of talcum powder, which was something he had once seen his grandpa putting down his pants.

"Sorry, M."

That was what his mum, who liked to give her children nicknames, sometimes called him instead of Malc. Malcolm was all right with that.

"He's a chinchilla," she continued.

"And not just any chinchilla!" said Stewart. "He's an Andean Lanigera!"

"Pardon?" said Malcolm.

"That's the breed. It means he's from the Andes, in South America. That's the best type! The ones that make perfect pets!!"

Malcolm looked down at the little creature.

It was mainly white, with bits of speckled grey round its nose. It had round, sticky-out ears and a big fluffy tail. It was sitting up on its back legs looking up at him, hopefully.

The chinchilla, like Malcolm, had very blue eyes. Those blue eyes seemed to widen as they saw Malcolm, like the animal had realised, instinctively, exactly whose pet it was meant to be.

Malcolm looked back at the chinchilla.

It could have been a special moment. A moment

when boy and chinchilla, chinchilla and boy, could really have bonded.

Time stretched, as blue

eyes met blue eyes, through the bars of the little cage.

But then, Malcolm turned away, shaking his head and tutting.

"Right… OK…" he said. "So where's… my Apache 321?!"

CHAPTER TWO

700 cats, 800 dogs and
five giraffes

"Your what?" said Malcolm's dad.

"My laptop that I asked for! I wrote it on my birthday list and everything!!"

"Sorry, Malcolm," said his mum, "what birthday list?"

"The one I stuck up on the kitchen wall!"

"Oh…" said Malcolm's sister, Libby, in her bored voice, which was the one she used most of the time, when not cooing over cute animals. "I think Ticky may have ripped that down a few days ago. When she was play-fighting with Tacky…"

"The cats ripped down my birthday list? So where is it now?"

"I think… Chewie may have eaten it…?" said his dad.

"The dog *ate* my birthday list?"

"Either the dog or the hamster."

"Marvin wouldn't eat that," said Grandpa. "Would play havoc with his digestion."

"Actually, I think I may have put it on the floor of the *iguana's* cage. Sorry, Malc… olm," said his mum. "Only I didn't realise that's what it was. I just thought it was some bits of paper. And you know how 'Nana likes to scratch around in bits of paper."

"But…" said Malcolm, getting more and more frustrated, "…we've already *got* loads of animals! We've got two cats, a dog, a hamster and an iguana. *Which most people would say is enough pets.*"

"M!" said Jackie. "You can't have enough pets."

"Exactly! I agree!" said Stewart.

"Yeah. YOLO," said Libby, who used a *lot* of these acronyms.

"Yes, siree!" said Grandpa Theo.

"I want to eat him!" said Bert.

Even the chinchilla seemed to nod, its enormous ears flapping up and down as it stared quizzically at Malcolm from inside its sparkling new cage, which had a water bottle attached to the outside, and a running wheel and a mirror inside.

"Right," said Malcolm. "Let's just look at that statement for a moment. You can't have enough pets. So… if we had 700 cats, and 800 dogs, and five – I don't know if you can keep them as pets, but I imagine if you *could*, you, Mum, would soon be off to the pet shop to get them – *giraffes*… would that be enough pets?"

"Well," said Stewart. "As long as they were all house-trained."

"I don't think we could get a litter tray big enough

for that many cats and dogs, Stewart," said Jackie. "To say nothing of the giraffes."

Grandpa frowned. "I wouldn't like to see a giraffe use a litter tray, even if it *was* big enough." He shook his head. "Bottoms too far off the ground."

"TD,"[1] said Libby.

"Hello?" said Malcolm. "Are we seriously discussing the pros and cons of getting 700 cats, 800 dogs and five giraffes now?"

But this question was never answered. Because the chinchilla – who later that day would be christened Chinny Reckon, by Stewart, after a funny phrase he used to say at school, in the 1970s – started running on the running wheel.

"OMGTT!"[2] said Libby, crouching down next to the cage. "That's soooooooooooo cute!!"

"Look at his little nose!" said Stewart.

---

[1] True Dat. As well as using all the standard acronyms, Libby made up a lot of her own.
[2] Oh My God Times Two.

"And his adorable enormous ears!" said Jackie.

"Actually, he doesn't look much like Lord Kitchener…" said Grandpa Theo.

"I want to eat him!" said Bert.

Eleven-year-old Malcolm watched the chinchilla running in its wheel for a moment. The chinchilla looked back at him, but kept running, almost as if it wanted Malcolm to be impressed.

"Look!" said Jackie. "He loves you!"

Malcolm looked at his family, clucking and cooing over the new pet. A part of him wanted to join them, to be in that group hug round the cage. But another part of him couldn't.

"Yes," said Malcolm quietly. "Thing is, I don't love *him*…" And, for extra emphasis (a bit like *The Terminator*, in one of Malcolm's favourite films, does when he says *Hasta la vista*), he said it again, but in Spanish, a language he had just started to learn at school: "*Yo no lo amo.*"

As ever, when he tried to tell his family how he felt about animals, no one seemed to hear him. So he sighed and turned away, and walked down the hallway towards his bedroom, passing on his way the family's two cats, Ticky and Tacky, their dog Chewie, their hamster Marvin and their iguana, Banana.

As it happened, someone in the living room *had* heard him. Someone with enormous ears; someone who could hear words even when they were said quietly. Someone who, when Malcolm said, *"Yo no lo amo,"* stopped running on his wheel, got off, and went and sat in the corner of the cage, facing the wall.

CHAPTER THREE

Mini-coloured Munch Balls

Malcolm lay back on his bed, looking out on to the street.[3] He could still, faintly, hear the sound of his family making cute noises round the cage – now added to by the *click-click-click* of his sister's phone, which meant that she was taking selfies, pouting, with the chinchilla in the background. He could also hear other, very tinny, animal noises, so he assumed

---

[3] They lived on a street called Kendal Road. House number 43. You might think this is a bit too much detail, but you'll be pleased I told you later on. Just you watch.

that Bert must have got hold of his dad's phone. Malcolm's family did not have much money:[4] his mum worked as a receptionist at the local vet's, and his dad designed apps, none of which had been very successful.

The only one that had got on to the Apple Store was called AnimalSFX, which was one where you pressed on some cartoon animals and it would make the sounds of those animals. No one really played with it any more, except Bert – which meant that along with all the other animal noises in the house, Malcolm could also hear an artificially created donkey, cow and elephant. This just made him more depressed.

He wondered why his family never got the message about him and animals. After all, he thought, looking round the room, his walls were

---

[4] Although Malcolm did sometimes think they might have more money if they spent less of it on *pets*.

the only ones in the house that didn't have animal pictures on them. Libby's and Bert's bedrooms were covered in cute images of kittens and puppies and seals and bears and penguins and – y'know: all the animals. His parents' bedroom didn't have animal posters on the wall, but they did have lots of family photographs, and every family photograph included the pets. Even Grandpa's room had a painting in it of some dogs playing poker.

Malcolm felt quite bad about it. He knew kids were supposed to like animals. He knew *people* were supposed to like animals. He knew that not liking animals generally made other people think that you were a bad person.

And, anyway, he didn't *not* like animals, really. He just didn't really *get* animals. Most of them seemed to lie around eating and sleeping and not doing anything useful.[5] He had watched

Ticky and Tacky (or possibly Tacky and Ticky – even though one was mainly brown and one was mainly white, Malcolm was always unsure which was which) for long periods of time and had never seen them, for example, read a book, or make a cake, or design a fantastic computer, or do any of the things he was interested in. Even now as he looked out of the window, he could see some pigeons in the street doing that stupid pigeon thing of hanging around in the middle of the road waiting until the last moment of a car approaching before flying away. Why did they do that?

But because his family so liked animals, and had so many animals, and went on so much about animals, sometimes – like now – he felt like he really

---

5 To be fair, though, one thing Malcolm shared with animals was that he did very much like sleep. Not only that, he was very good at sleeping, able to go to sleep really easily. And not just in bed, but wherever he fancied it: in the car, on the sofa, and more than a few times, in his school classroom. This is also important information for later on.

did not like animals. He sometimes wondered, in fact, if his mum and dad preferred animals to children; or at least to him, their one child who wasn't obsessed with animals.

At those moments, he sometimes felt like he hated animals. He didn't like to admit that, but he knew that at those moments it was true.

There was a knock on the door.

Malcolm didn't answer.

"Malc," came his mum's voice, from behind the door.

"Mum!" he said.

"Sorry, M! Are you OK? Are you asleep?"

"Clearly not," replied Malcolm.

"That makes a change," she said.

"Can we come in?" said Stewart.

"Is the chinchilla with you?"

Malcolm heard some whispers, some scuttling and the sound of a cage door being locked.

"No…" said Stewart, eventually.

"OK," said Malcolm.

The door opened and his family shuffled in, holding out, like peace offerings, Malcolm's other presents.[6]

Malcolm, immediately forgiving them for the chinchilla, greedily opened them.

They were:

- *Caring For a Chinchilla*: A Guide
- Chinchilla Treats, 5 kg
- Mini-coloured Munch Balls (for chinchillas). Five of them, all different colours

Controlling himself – quite well, at first – Malcolm looked up from these presents and said: "Thanks. No, really: thanks. I really appreciate it. Um… anything… not to do with chinchillas?"

---

[6] Apart from Libby, who was holding her phone.

Jackie and Stewart exchanged glances.

"Um… of course!" said Stewart, handing over another present. Malcolm unwrapped it, suspiciously. Then held up what was inside and looked at his parents.

"It's a chinchilla," he said. "A cuddly toy chinchilla."

"No…" said Jackie. "I'd say it's a… rabbit. Wouldn't you, Dad?"

"Yes! Or maybe… a… a… big-eared hamster!"

"Right, yes. A big-eared hamster. Maybe we should call it… um…"

"Hammy Big-Ears!" said Stewart.

"LOLTT…"[7] said Libby.

"Exactly!" said Jackie. "Hello, Hammy Big-Ears! Look at your cute… big… hamster ears!"

"Right," said Malcolm. "So when you bought this cuddly toy, you weren't sure what kind of animal it was meant to be? It had no label of any kind?

---

[7] I'll leave you to work this one out.

It wasn't in any particular section of the cuddly toy shop? Perhaps the CH section? Just after Cheetahs and Chimpanzees?"

"Can I eat it?" said Bert.

"I think that clinches it," said Malcolm, tossing the toy to Bert. "It's a chinchilla."

And, with that, he lay back on his bed, with his arms crossed, looking up at the ceiling. "Mum, Dad," whispered Libby. "You know why Malcolm's like this, DC?"[8] She lowered her voice to an even lower whisper, made lower still because of her bored voice, which was like someone speaking through a yawn. "It's cos of the Monkey Moment. IKEA…"[9]

"No, it's not," said Malcolm. The whisper had clearly not been whispery enough.

Jackie and Stewart exchanged glances. "It probably is, isn't it, Stewart?" Jackie whispered.

---

[8] Don't Cha?

[9] I Know Everything Always.

"Yes, darling, I think we all know it is…" Stewart whispered back. "I think because of the…"

"…Monkey Moment," said Jackie.

"Yes, the Monkey Moment… Perhaps Malcolm still feels a bit traumatised around furry creatures…"

"The whispers aren't working!" said Malcolm. "I can hear you! It's a small room! And: it's got nothing to do with the Monkey Moment! Stop saying the words 'Monkey Moment'!"

"What 'Monkey Moment'?" said Grandpa.

"Oh, Dad! We've told you a hundred times!" said Jackie.

"Tell me again," said Grandpa. "You know how I forget things."

Malcolm sighed, and looked out of the window at a pigeon flying away from a car bumper at the last second.

CHAPTER FOUR

The Monkey Moment

So the family told Grandpa again. Thoughtfully, they went back into the living room and left Malcolm in his bedroom, as they didn't want him to have to relive the trauma of the Monkey Moment, even if he said he wasn't traumatised by it.

"Well, Dad," said Jackie, "when Malcolm was six, we went on one of our regular Sunday trips to the zoo. And he loved seeing the animals then, didn't he, Stewart?"

"Yes," said Stewart. "I remember him running up and down by all the cages, smiling his biggest smile."

"So the animals he *really* wanted to see were the monkeys…"

"Fair dos," said Grandpa. "They are the top animal in a zoo."

Everyone nodded in agreement.

"And when we got there – to the monkey house…"

"Monkey house, yes," said Grandpa.

"He was really excited!"

"CGI…" said Libby, nodding in agreement, but in a way that suggested that she could barely be bothered to nod.

"What does that one mean?" said Grandpa.

"Crazy Gagging for It…"

"Right you are."

"And so he ran right up to the cage. The one with all the chimpanzees in it. And the chimpanzees were all rolling about and swinging from ropes and jumping through tyres and chasing each other along the tree trunks…"

"Sounds great!" said Grandpa.

"Can I eat them?" said Bert.

"And Malcolm loved it all. He was so happy. He loved it so much, in fact, that he started clapping."

At this point, Jackie paused, and looked a bit troubled.

"Yes," said Grandpa. "Then what happened? Don't stop there: INTK!"[10]

"Well…" said Jackie, "when Malcolm clapped, all the chimpanzees stopped what they were doing. And then one of the biggest ones… the dominant male, I think…"

"Louie," said Stewart, helpfully. "That was his name. I remember reading it on the little placard

---

[10] I Need To Know. Grandpa had picked up some of Libby's acronyms.

outside the cage. They'd got him from a zoo in Frankfurt."

"Yes, all right, Louie… He…" For a moment, it looked like Jackie was going to cry. Stewart came over and put his arm round her; Libby yawned; Bert found a piece of fluff on the floor and put it in his mouth.

"You don't have to continue if you don't want to, darling," said Stewart.

"No, it's fine. I'll be fine." She took a deep breath. "Louie picked up some of his… poo. From the floor. And threw it in Malcolm's face."

Grandpa nodded, with a very serious expression.

Then he nodded some more, making his face even more serious.

Then… he started laughing.

"Grandpa!" said Stewart.

"Sorry, but…" He couldn't carry on the sentence. He started gulping for breath in between the laughs.

"The monkey plop splattered on the bars of the cage," said Jackie. "But that didn't stop him getting it all over his face. It's not funny! It was awful!"

Grandpa carried on laughing. Then Stewart started. Then Bert joined in, while also repeatedly pressing the monkey icon on AnimalSFX on Stewart's phone to create the sound of a chattering monkey. Even Libby stopped looking bored and started smiling.

"Stop it! Why are you all laughing?!" said Jackie. "And then – and then – all the other chimps joined in!"

"AHHAHAHAHA!!"

That was everybody else, laughing.

"LOLT27!!"

"Stop it!" said Jackie. "They all looked round – twenty chimps – and they all picked up bits of poo – and *all* threw it at the same time at Malcolm! It was like a huge battalion of medieval soldiers catapulting cannonballs at a castle! Except it wasn't medieval

soldiers, it was monkeys! And it wasn't a castle, it was Malcolm's face! And it wasn't cannonballs, it was… AHHHHHAHAHAHA…!!!"

That, unfortunately, was Jackie. Joining in with the laughter.

"…poo…!!" she finally finished.

"AHHHHHAHAHAHA!!!"

"It was poo!" she said again, irrelevantly, to be honest. "Monkey droppings! Chimp plop! Planet of the Apes poo-poo! AHHHHHAHAHAHA!!"

"AHHHAHAHAHA!!"

That was everyone else.

"So… having a nice time?" That was Malcolm.

Everyone looked round.

Malcolm was standing at the door to the living room, with his arms crossed.

The rest of the family fell silent.

For almost twelve seconds.

Then they all started laughing again. In that

way that people do when they're trying not to, laughter bursting out of them like jets of air from an overfull balloon that someone is releasing, then pinching closed, and then releasing again. It's made worse, that type of laughter, if you're the object of it, because it sounds like the people laughing are not just laughing at you, but blowing raspberries as well.

"BRRRR! HAHAHA!! HAHAHA! BRRRR! AHHAHAHAHA!!!" went Malcolm's family.

Chatter chatter chatter scream scream scream! went AnimalSFX in Bert's hand.

Malcolm shook his head, raised his eyes to heaven and turned to go back to his bedroom.

"Hang on, Malcolm," said Stewart. "Sorry sorry sorry! We're all really sorry! Aren't we?"

"Yes!" said Jackie.

"Yes!" said Grandpa.

"STTM…"[11] said Libby.

"Can I eat sorry?" said Bert.

"But look…" said Stewart. "If it helps… we do have one more present."

"Is it a chinchilla hat?" said Malcolm, not turning round. "A chinchilla key-ring? Tickets to *Chin-Chinniny Chinniny-Chinniny Chin-Chin Chilla!: The Musical?*"

"No!"

"It's got nothing to do with chinchillas at all…?"

"Nothing."

Slowly, Malcolm turned round. He looked at his father suspiciously.

"All right then," he said.

---

[11] Soz To The Max.

CHAPTER FIVE

The last present

Stewart walked over to Malcolm, then took something out of his pocket and handed it over.

The last present.

It was slim: perhaps some kind of card, wrapped up in the candles paper.

Aha! thought Malcolm. *A voucher! I can use that to buy the Apache 321!*

"Oh, thanks, Dad!" he said, as his fingers took off the Sellotape on the back. "And Mum! Sorry, I didn't mean to be ungrateful about the chinchilla! Can we go to the shops today with the vouch—"

Malcolm stopped speaking, as the word *vouch* ended on his lips, never to be added to with an *er*. He frowned, looking at the piece of card, on which were many, many pictures of animals.

For the second time that day, Malcolm looked up in confusion at his beaming parents.

"It's a card! That we all made together!" said Libby. "BT!"[12]

"Oh… that's nice…"

"Look inside," said Jackie. "We saved up!"

Malcolm looked inside. There were more pictures of animals, plus the words, "Happy Birthday!"

There was also a piece of paper, folded up. *Ah*, he thought, *the voucher. Right.*

Malcolm unfolded the piece of paper.

---

[12] Be Thankful.

It wasn't a voucher.

It was an invoice.[13] An invoice from his school: he knew this because the words Bracket Wood Primary School were printed on top of it.[14] On the main bit of the paper were the words:

YEAR SIX SCHOOL TRIP

With a stamp across them that said:

PAID

Malcolm looked up.

"Oh. Thanks!"

He meant this, even though it wasn't a voucher

---

[13] An invoice, in case you don't know, is a bit of paper grown-ups give each other when they've bought something, to show that they've bought it. If you did know, I'm sorry I told you again.

[14] Although the B and the K and a bit of the P were faded out, as the Bracket Wood Primary School printer had run out of ink. Four years ago.

that he could use to buy an FZY Apache 321. Malcolm knew that his mum and dad would have struggled to pay the £300 required for the Year Six School Trip. In fact, as he looked at the invoice, it occurred to him that possibly it was a good thing that Ticky and Tacky had torn down his birthday list – and it had then been spread on the bottom of 'Nana's cage – as maybe, he realised now, his mum and dad couldn't actually afford an FZY Apache 321.

And Malcolm *did* want to go: the Year Six Trip was exciting. It was three days long – the first time he'd be away from his family! – and most other children he knew would be going. So he would've sounded more enthusiastic about his thanks were it not for the fact that he didn't actually know where the school trip was going to this year.

So he said:

"No, really, Mum and Dad, thanks. That's really

nice of you. By the way – I know I should know this, but – where is it to, this year? The trip?"

"Um…" said Jackie and Stewart, both at the same time.

ONE WEEK LATER

CHAPTER SIX

We're here!

The Bracket Wood Primary School coach was having trouble getting down the hill.

This might seem unusual: you would expect most vehicles as old and creaky as the Bracket Wood Primary School coach to have trouble getting *up* this particular hill, a hill in the middle of the countryside renowned for its steepness. And of course it *had* done when it had driven up the other side – the climb had taken an hour and a half, and at one point most of

Year Six had started screaming, "It's going to roll backwards! It's going to roll backwards!" and cowering under their seats.

But once over the top, even the rustiest rustbucket should be able just to glide all the way down. As it was, though, it seemed less to glide than to… cough. And splutter.

None of this was helped by the weather, which, though it was spring, was rainy and foggy.

Malcolm sighed, closed his eyes and tried to rest his forehead on the shuddering window. Up ahead he could see a flock of sheep running away from them as the coach belched its way forward. The vehicle finally managed to gain some speed and pass the sheep, but Malcolm noticed that they carried on running, even though there was nothing behind them any more. In fact, that they were now basically chasing the bus they were supposed to be running away from.

Some boys at the back – a boy called Barry, and his friends Lukas, Jake and Taj – turned round to point at the sheep, running away from nothing, and laughed. But Malcolm just felt annoyed at the stupid stupidity of the stupid sheep.

Eventually they made it to the bottom of the hill, and their destination.

"We're here!" said their teacher, Mr Barrington, peering out of the front window. "I think…"

He said "I think" partly because his eyesight was not of the best – he had very, very thick glasses –

and partly because the sign he was looking at was obscured by mist.

But *as* he said "I think", the mist cleared to reveal the words:

ORWELL FARM

"Yes, this is definitely the place," he said. "Drive on, driver, quick-smart! Let's waste no more time getting the children *out* of this bus, *on to* the farm, and starting to look after all the animals!"

"Hooray!!" went all the children.

Well, all except one.

CHAPTER SEVEN

Stinky Blinky

"So! Everybody! The last animals on our tour – and the last animals you'll be helping us to look after while you're here – are... the goats!"

Gavin, who ran Orwell Farm and who had been giving Year Six their first trip round it, proudly gestured towards the pen behind him. All the children – except for Malcolm – peered towards the animals.

"Does anyone know what we get from goats?" continued Gavin.

A girl called Ellie put her hand up.

"Yes?" said Gavin.

"Milk?"

"That's right!"

"I thought *cows* produced milk?" said her twin brother Fred.

"And burgers!" said Morris Fawcett, who was also in Year Six, although some people thought he should go back to Year One where he would almost certainly be more comfortable.

"They don't *produce* burgers, Morris," said Morris's sister, Isla.

Morris frowned. "I thought beef comes from cows."

"It does."

Morris frowned even more. "Well, how do they *make* it then?"

Gavin smiled, which made his beard (he had a big bushy beard, and wore a flat cap, even though he was quite young) go up at the sides. "We get milk from goats as well. We make our speciality cheese out of it!"

Maven, who may or may not have been Gavin's wife but who ran the farm with him, held up a plate on which rested a big triangular piece of what looked like rotting soap.

"Stinky Blinky!"

"Urrgh!" said various children. Even though they were out in the open air, a few of them covered their mouths and noses so as to avoid the terrible scent of cheesy goat wee.

"We sell it at the local artisan market!" said

Maven. "Goes like hot cakes! Who wants a bit?"

The children all looked down.

Malcolm, though, was already looking down, at his watch. The time was 5.43pm. He had known that for a while (well, at least since it was 5.42pm). But he wasn't looking at his watch to find out what the time was. He was looking at his watch because he wasn't interested in what Gavin or Maven were saying about the goats.

He hadn't been interested in what Gavin or Maven had said about the chickens either; or the sheep;[15] or the cows; or the horses; or the sheepdog, Trotsky; or the farm cat, Zsa-Zsa; or the tortoises, Benny and Bjorn, which they kept not because they were farm animals, but just, in Gavin's words, "for giggles".[16]

---

[15] Actually, Malcolm had thought about asking Gavin why it is that sheep will continue to run away from something they think is chasing them even after it's gone past them – to the point that they will then be chasing the thing they're supposed to be running away from – but he decided he couldn't be bothered.

[16] He started to say another word before "giggles", but Maven shushed him.

He – Malcolm – still couldn't see the point. The animals just walked or sat around in their pens looking at the humans while the humans looked back at them. It was like a very dull episode of *Big Brother*. Which was a show he never watched because it was very dull.

No, Malcolm wasn't looking at his watch to check the time.

He was looking at his watch to check the date.

And thinking: *Three days. Three days till I can go home.*

Meanwhile, Gavin and Maven had walked over to either side of one of the goats. It was a very old-looking goat, with a very long tufty beard, not entirely unlike Gavin's. It had a sad face, and bulging amber eyes.

"This old guy, though…" Gavin said, "he's our favourite. He might even be our favourite animal on the entire farm."

"We call him K-Pax," said Maven. "Do any of you kids know that movie?"

Year Six, collectively, shook their heads.

"Oh, it's *great*," said Gavin. "We love it."

"Yuh! So we, like, found K-Pax when we were trekking in the Himalayas!" said Maven. "And the village were going to, like, slaughter him. Which would've been…"

"Gross!"

"Yeah, gross."

"I mean, they weren't even going to sell the meat organically at the local market or anything…"

"So…" said Maven, "we bought him. And shipped him back to live with us here at Orwell Farm!"

Malcolm raised his eyes from his watch. They felt heavy with boredom.

"Anyway," Gavin continued, "because he's so old, and he's seen so much of the world, we think K-Pax is really wise and clever! So if any of you have any questions – any big life issues you've been wondering about – ask them now!"

There was a long pause. Year Six, collectively, looked back down at the ground. Not because Maven was still holding up the Stinky Blinky – although she was – but because all the children were a bit embarrassed about the idea of asking a goat a question. Malcolm shook his head and imagined it.

Hello, K-Pax. Can you please tell me what life holds for me? Should I follow my dreams of being a great inventor of computer games or settle for being someone whose apps never get made, like my dad?

Sorry, what's that you say? Baaa? Baaa-Baaa? Oh, and you've done a stinky goat wee. Great. Thanks.

"Right!" said Gavin. "First tour over! Everybody back to the farmhouse for…"

Malcolm finally looked up. At least there would be nice food. And he was peckish.

"…Stinky Blinky sandwiches!!" said Maven.

CHAPTER EIGHT

K-Pax

Led by Gavin and Maven, Year Six shuffled off towards the farmhouse, which was an old, thatched building, encircled by all the various animal pens.

Malcolm, suddenly less peckish, watched them go. He let out a deep sigh. At this moment, three days felt very long indeed.

"Hey, Malcolm, you coming?" said Barry.

"Yeah," said Malcolm, about to join his classmates when he stopped. Because he had a weird sense that someone was watching him. He looked around, but couldn't see anyone. He shrugged, and tried to think nothing of it… but no, he could feel eyes on him, somewhere.

Then, he realised where.

Straight in front of him: the goat.

K-Pax had come over to the edge of the pen and was leaning his head over the small fence. His bulging amber eyes were, it seemed, *trained* on Malcolm. *Staring* at him.

"Stop looking at me like that," said Malcolm.

But K-Pax didn't. He kept looking. *Well, of course he's still looking*, thought Malcolm. *He's an animal, and one of the* most *boring things about animals is that they don't speak English.*[17]

So Malcolm tutted, and stared right back into K-Pax's eyes.

---

[17] Or any other language. Spanish, for example. Malcolm may have had issues with animals, but he was definitely not racist.

"OK. Tell you what," he said, "let's pretend that Gavin and Maven are right, and you, K-Pax, are really, really wise. Then answer me this. Every other kid in the world loves animals. Every other *person* in the world, it seems, loves animals. But I don't. I'm sorry. I don't mean to offend you, or any other of your furry friends, but I... I just can't see the point of you."

During this speech, K-Pax just carried on listening imperviously, occasionally munching on some much-chewed-up grass. If he was offended, he didn't, it has to be said, show it. He continued simply to stare into Malcolm's eyes.

Malcolm, even though he knew it was silly, got a strange feeling that the goat was *actually* staring at him: staring into his soul. He didn't want to feel that – he particularly didn't want to feel that about an animal, who he knew couldn't possibly be doing it – so he made a point of leaning in even closer to K-Pax's snouty white face.

"So, K-Pax, my question is: why is that? Why *don't* I love animals? And more importantly, how – in order to be like everyone else – am I ever going to learn *how* to love them?"

After Malcolm asked this question, K-Pax seemed, for a second, to shut his eyes, almost – almost – as if he was thinking about it. But it was so quick, it may have been a blink. And when he opened them again, his eyes looked bigger and bulgier than ever.

It had actually felt quite a relief for Malcolm to finally say this stuff out loud. These were things he felt very deeply, but most of the time kept to himself. But once it was out, and the goat was just looking back at him, Malcolm thought:

This is just stupid. I may as well be talking to a brick wall.

Plus there was quite a strong scent of Stinky Blinky coming from… well, Malcolm didn't really want to think about where it was coming from. So he started to back away.

Except he couldn't. It was weird. It was like he was rooted to the spot. The ground was a bit dirty around the pen – maybe his wellies had sunk into the mud?

He made to look down at his feet – but he couldn't do that either. He couldn't, in fact, take his eyes away from K-Pax's eyes.

It was like he was being hypnotised. By a goat. This seemed very unlikely to Malcolm, seeing as perhaps the one thing he knew for certain about goats was that none of them had trained in hypnotherapy.

But certain things about the situation really did seem like hypnotism.

Other eyes looking deep into your eyes, while you look into them, for example; not being able to look away; and... this was probably the big one... suddenly feeling...

...very... very...

...slee..............

CHAPTER NINE

Kind of green

When Malcolm woke up, on the grass near the goat pen, he felt a little odd. For a start, he felt very tired. Or at least… he felt like all his limbs were much heavier than normal, and that moving his head – or his arms, or his legs – was a real effort. His body in particular felt weighed down, like there was something hefty on his back, pressing him into the grass.

But he had occasionally felt a bit like this waking

up at home when he'd gone to bed late. Plus his dad had once described to him feeling *exactly* like this when *he* woke up.[18]

So maybe, Malcolm thought, *I've just slept badly. Which would make sense, seeing as how I hadn't been planning on going to sleep at all. Last thing I remember was that stupid old goat staring at me, and then — well — I must have passed out. No wonder I feel weird.*

He tried to see where the goat had gone, but he couldn't, for some reason, see much at all. Every time he lifted his head, all he could see were the tips of the grass and just the bottom edge of the goat pen. He strained his neck as high as it could go — it felt, strangely, like he could in fact stretch his neck further up from his shoulders than usual — but he still couldn't see more than a foot or so above the ground.

---

[18] Although that had been the morning after a night when he'd been out at the pub. So that *may* have had something to do with it.

Well, of course, Malcolm thought, *it's because I'm lying down. I can feel my tummy and hands and legs on the grass. On, it must be said, the wet and muddy grass. So let's stand up.*

This turned out to be much more difficult than usual. Try as he might, Malcolm couldn't seem to get off all fours. He pushed and pushed with his arms, trying to get himself up, but nothing doing. It was exhausting.

One more push, he thought. *One big heave.*

He summoned up all his strength, and started, yes, genuinely started to get up – he even, for a second, saw a tiny bit of goat horn peeping over the pen fence – before tumbling over and ending up on his back.

And then it *really* seemed impossible to get up. Lying on his back, looking up at the sky, all he seemed to be able to do, however much he tried, was wobble from side to side. He felt like a Weeble.

His arms and legs were gyrating, uselessly, in the air. He must look, he thought, like a beetle or a cockroach when they get stuck on their backs.

It was at this point Malcolm noticed something about his arms, which were the only limbs he could actually see. He noticed that they were... kind of *green*. And kind of... elephantine. Not in the sense of large. More in the sense of small, but really like an elephant's. Which was odd, seeing as the main thing about elephants is that they are big.

So, he thought – mainly to think about something so as not to just start screaming in terror – what *isn't* an elephant but has legs and arms a bit like an elephant's, only much smaller... plus when they roll over they can't turn back again... plus is: green?

He felt like the answer was right there, just beyond his reach.

"Hello..." said a deep, low voice next to his ear. "You in a bit of a pickle, mate?"

Malcolm looked round to see where the voice was coming from. Despite everything else he might have thought at that moment when he saw where it was indeed coming from, what he actually thought was: *of course*.

That's what's smaller than an elephant but with similar-shaped arms and legs and gets stuck on its back and is green.

A *tortoise*.

And then, finally, he screamed in terror.

CHAPTER TEN

Option C

About a minute later, Malcolm stopped screaming. *Maybe I imagined it all*, he thought.

He closed his eyes tight, and opened them again.

Then he looked at his wrinkly green arms, and thought about how he'd rolled on to his back and got stuck there.

He craned forward, and saw a section of something that was clearly on his back. It looked a bit like a World War Two German soldier's helmet – only greener – and more, well, shell-like. *Tortoise*-shell like.

Then he started screaming again.

The tortoise – the one who wasn't Malcolm – just watched him curiously the whole time. Then he said:

"Well, it's not *that* bad."

"Yes, it is!!" said Malcolm. "I'm a tortoise! I'm a tortoise!"

"I know *that*. But it's happened to all of us at some point…"

"Has it?"

Malcolm, through his fear, felt a glimmer of hope. It happens to lots of people? This tortoise was also a human who had somehow ended up a tortoise? Of course! That's why he could speak! Then there must be a way back to being hu—

"Hey!" he said, as the tortoise broke Malcolm's train of thought by nuzzling his snout somewhere under Malcolm's shell.

"Hang on!" said the tortoise.

"Hang on to whaa—" said Malcolm, as he felt himself being lifted on to his side. And then perched on his side. He rotated slightly like a very slowly spinning coin. The tortoise backed away, and retreated inside his shell.

"What are you doing?" said Malcolm. "Don't leave me on the edge! On the edge of my… edge!"

"Just taking a breather," said the tortoise, emerging from his shell. "You're not exactly terrapin-sized, are you? And besides, I need you to keep spinning round until I'm facing your shell-side."

"Can't you walk round to my…" Malcolm couldn't believe he was saying it, "…shell-side?!"

The tortoise blinked. "Do you want to stay like that until next year?"

"Er…"

"No. Thought not."

Malcolm continued to revolve. Helplessly, he watched as the tortoise disappeared from view.

"Right!" said the tortoise's voice. "Try and stay like that. I'll take a bit of a run-up."

About fifteen minutes passed.

During those fifteen minutes, Malcolm thought about what on earth could have happened. These were the options as he saw them.

A) He was dreaming. But he didn't think this could be right, as he normally only dreamt about computers. And *never* about animals. Plus, it really didn't feel like a dream.

B) He was having some kind of hallucination, brought on by extreme boredom following a whole day – a whole life, it felt like – of people telling him about animals.

C) He had turned into a tortoise.

He was mainly going with option B, option A being dismissed for the reasons explained within option A, and option C, being, um, not possible.

Either way, he thought, it was best to just go along with what was happening, and assume that, eventually, everything could be got back to normal. The only alternative, after all, was screaming in horror, and there was a limit to how long he could do that for.

Then Malcolm felt a bump as the other tortoise finally reached him.

Gradually, more or less at the speed that the Bailey family car-boot door shut when not slammed, he came back down: the right way up.

"Oooofff!" he said. He looked to his left. The tortoise was still there.

"Thanks," said Malcolm, because that was what the tortoise looked like he was expecting.

"No worries." The tortoise, satisfied, began to

turn round.

"Sorry… um…?"

"Benny."

"Benny? You're one of the farm tortoises…? With Bjorn?"

"Yes. Course. I'm not a *wild* tortoise."

Malcolm frowned, although that wasn't something that was easily noticeable. Basically, his face just went a little more wrinkly than usual.

"Are there such things?"

"Not in the UK, no."

"Um…" said Malcolm. "You said – earlier – that it happens to all of us…"

"Well, it does."

"How do you get out of it, then?"

Benny looked at him. "Like I just showed you."

"What did you show me?"

"How to *get out of* being stuck on your back!"

Malcolm shook his head. Even that, he was

aware, took quite a bit of time.

"No! I thought you meant *get out of* being a tortoise. How do you get out of being a *tortoise!*"

"Oh," said Benny. "Can't help you there, I'm afraid."

Which was when Malcolm started screaming again.

CHAPTER ELEVEN

Benny and Bjorn

"But I don't want to be a tortoise!" said Malcolm, when he finally stopped screaming.

"Excuse me!" said another voice, sounding very cross. Malcolm and Benny looked round.

It was another tortoise.

"That's a *terrible* thing to say!" the other tortoise said, in a higher voice than Benny's. "Why would you not want to be a tortoise? It's a wonderful thing to be!"

"No, it isn't," said Benny.

"Shut up," said the new tortoise.

"It's a bit depressing sometimes. You know, when a frightening thing happens, like a fox appears, or a loud noise, and you stick your head inside your shell – sometimes you can be in there for hours, not sure whether or not to come out…"

"Only if you're a scaredy-tortoise, like you!"

"Although I like the long sleeping part," said Benny. "That's nice."

"Bjorn, I presume," said Malcolm, to the new tortoise.

"Yes. However, I prefer Bjornita…"

"Oh. You're like a girl tortoise born in a boy-tortoise body?"

"No. I'm just a girl tortoise. And Gavin knew that as well, when they named me!"

"So why did they call you Bjorn?"

Bjornita raised her eyes, almost as if she had eyebrows.

"They thought calling the two of us after the two human men in Abba was *hilarious*."

"I mean, personally…" said Benny, "I think if you're going to do that kind of joke, there are other options…"

"*Sonny and Cher!*" said Bjornita. "It's obvious! You could have been Sonny, I could've been Cher…"

"Sorry, who?" said Malcolm.

"Sonny and… you mean you've never heard of…? Oh well. They were a singing duo in the 1960s – married – well, for a bit. She was a hippie, and he was—"

"How do you know all this stuff?" said Malcolm, interrupting what looked like it was going to be a fairly long description of the career of Sonny and Cher.

Bjornita and Benny looked at each other.

"Well," said Benny, "we *are* 150 years old."

"Speak for yourself!" said Bjornita. "I'm not a day over 148."

"No, I mean," said Malcolm, "how… Wait, really? You're really 148 years old?"

"Are you saying I'm lying?" said Bjornita, looking hurt.[19]

"No…" said Malcolm.

"Well, to be fair, Bjornita, you are," said Benny.

"So I'm 149!" she said. "So sue me!!"

"No, what I meant was – how do you know about human stuff?"

"Oh," said Benny. "Humans. They think animals can't understand what they're talking about."

"Well," said Bjornita, "except for when they say things like 'Come here, Benny; come here, Bjorn – lettuce, look, lovely lettuce…' They think we understand *that*. Frankly, though, I find it patronising. Talking to us like we're children."

"I guess it must be," said Malcolm. "Especially

---

[19] Well, about as hurt as a tortoise can look, which isn't that much. They always look a little bit in pain, don't they? Like they're groaning under the weight of their own shell.

when you're actually 149 years old."

"148!"

"You already admitted your age," whispered Benny.

"Oh yes," said Bjornita.

"Anyway," said Malcolm, "so you're telling me you've *never* been humans? And so you *don't* know any way for me to get back to being a human?"

Benny and Bjornita looked at each other.

"Sorry, walk that very slowly past me again?" said Benny, turning back to Malcolm.

Malcolm frowned.[20] "Don't you mean *run* that past me again?"

Benny looked at him. "I'm a tortoise."

"Oh, I see," said Malcolm. "Well. That's what I've been trying to tell you. I'm *not* a tortoise."

---

[20] Again, he didn't frown quite like he would've done with his human face. He couldn't, seeing as a tortoise face looks sort of like they're frowning most of the time. So from now on, whenever I describe Malcolm's face doing anything – frowning, smiling, raising an eyebrow – assume it's happening *inside*.

Benny and Bjornita stared at him, at his green skin and bald head and little elephant-y limbs and large, hard shell. "Are you *sure* about that?" said Bjornita.

"Yes. I'm a boy. A human boy. My name is Malcolm."

"Really?"

Benny and Bjornita seemed to suppress laughter. They shook a little inside their shells.

"Are you laughing?"

"No."

"You're shaking inside your shells."

"That's a tortoise thing," said Benny.

"You'll get used to it..." said Bjornita, "... Malcolm!!"

"No, you *are* laughing! It's a bit hard to tell because your tortoise faces don't really smile, but you are!"

"All right, we are," said Bjornita. Benny, embarrassed, had put his head inside his shell.

"So stop!"

"OK."

"And Benny. Come out again!"

He did.

"So. Listen. Please. The fact is: I'm not a tortoise. Or at least, I'm not *usually* a tortoise. I was just talking to that goat—"

"Talking to a goat? So – were you a goat? As well as a human?" said Bjornita, a bit sarcastically.

"No, I was talking to the goat when I was a human. In human language. I wasn't thinking that the goat understood. I was just telling the goat, in fact, that I—"

"Which goat was it?" said Benny, suddenly.

"Which goat? Um… What was he called again?"

Malcolm tried to remember. Suddenly, that felt difficult: as if everything that had happened up to the point of him becoming a tortoise was… disappearing from his memory. For a second, he started to wonder if what he was saying was wrong, if he had ever been a human at all.

And that felt even more frightening than anything else that had happened so far.

CHAPTER TWELVE

A sudden chill

But then it came back to him.

"K-Pax! The old one!"

Benny nodded. Bjornita nodded.

"What?" said Malcolm.

"Well…" whispered Benny, "there's a rumour here on the farm… that K-Pax… can *do* stuff…"

"Like what?"

"Weird stuff," said Bjornita, also in a whisper.

"Magic stuff?"

"Yes. Because, sometimes, right…" said Benny, leaning forward, and speaking even more quietly, and looking round, as if they were being watched, "…he *baas*. Like a sheep!"

"And…" said Bjornita, leaning in to what was now a very close triangle of tortoise heads, "I've heard that some of the lady goats in there – because of him – can make milk! Like a cow!"

Malcolm nodded. He took a deep breath.

"Yes. Sorry. None of that is magic."

"It isn't?" said Benny.

"No, it's just what goats do."

"How do you know?" said Bjornita. "We're just going by what we've heard. Because we can't see over the fence."

"No. But I can. I was looking over the fence earlier today. WHEN I WAS A BOY!!"

Benny and Bjornita looked to each other.

"Maybe… maybe he's telling the truth, Benny."

"Yes. Maybe he is, Bjorn."

"…ita."

"Oh. Yes. Sorry, sometimes even I forget."

"Well, as I said," said Bjornita, "being a tortoise is not such a terrible thing to be. But… if it's true that you are a boy, I can see how it might seem…"

"Terrible," said Benny. "Absolutely awful."

"Shut up," she said. Then she looked at Malcolm, who was hanging his little tortoise head. Bjornita, though quite high and mighty, was not without compassion.

"Listen, Malcolm," she said, "I'm sure we can find a way out of this. The first question to ask is: *why* have you been changed into a tortoise? What were you saying to K-Pax?"

Malcolm cast his mind back. Again, it took a bit more of an effort to remember than he'd thought it would, given it wasn't that long ago. But then the words reappeared in his mind.

"I was saying to him that I didn't really like – that I didn't know why I didn't like – and if there was any way of getting to like…"

Malcolm trailed off. Benny and Bjornita looked at him, quizzically.[21]

"Look," Malcolm said, "never mind *exactly* what I said to K-Pax. I just need to know if there's anything I can do – anything I need to do – to break the spell."

"What happened next? After you spoke to him?" said Benny.

"I don't know. I fell asleep."

"Well, maybe that's *it!*"

"What is?"

"You changed into a tortoise when you fell asleep. So maybe you'll change back into a human if you fall asleep again…?"

Malcolm thought about this. He had no clue if

---

[21] I know. All animals look kind of quizzical all the time. Just go with it.

it was right. Apart from anything, it was, after all, an idea being suggested to him by a tortoise. And y'know: even someone who really liked animals to begin with – even his mum, or dad, or sister – might not necessarily think that the answer to really difficult and mysterious questions lay with Benny the tortoise.

But he didn't have any other ideas. So, he shrugged his shoulders[22] and closed his eyes.

Then he heard a loud slam. And the ground began to shake.

---

[22] He didn't. Tortoises don't have shoulders. He just kind of wiggled.

CHAPTER THIRTEEN

Manky lettuce

Immediately, Benny and Bjornita's heads went inside their shells.

"What's happening?!" said Malcolm, opening his eyes wide.

Nothing. No response. It was like talking to two khaki domes. Or two rather mossy rocks. The ground shook more and more loudly.

"Benny! Bjornita!!" said Malcolm, panicked. "What should I do?!"

Still nothing. The ground was now shaking a lot, and Malcolm could hear a noise.

TRAMP. TRAMP. TRAMP.

Oh my God! he thought. And then suddenly, he knew what to do.

He darted his head inside his shell.

Inside, it was dark and quiet. He could still hear the **TRAMP TRAMP TRAMP** from outside, but it was much more like TRAMP TRAMP TRAMP. It was a bit like being inside a tent: kind of cosy, but rather cramped. And obviously stiffer than a tent:[23] his shell did not flap in the wind. It was echoey as well – he could hear his breath sounding loud in his ears.

What was strange – well, it was *all* strange, but this was *particularly* strange – was that although he knew his head was inside the shell, the hole to the outside looked like it was where his head

---

[23] The Baileys had gone camping last summer, which Malcolm hadn't enjoyed much, as they'd taken all the animals; he'd ended up with the iguana on top of his face in the morning.

should be. Like his head had been cut off, even though he knew it couldn't have been, as he was looking at the hole with his eyes, which were in his head.

Luckily, he wasn't able to carry on thinking about this, because then, somewhat muffled, he heard a voice say:

"Come here, Benny! Come here, Bjorn!"

This was followed by the sound of something being scattered on the ground. Through the hole in his shell, Malcolm saw three bits of manky lettuce and an ancient cucumber lying there. From his point of view, these vegetables looked very large; the manky lettuce leaves looked like bushes. Also they smelt, these vegetables, *strong* – much stronger than he would've expected. And he found himself drawn, via this smell – this strong smell of old vegetables, which was not something, to be honest, that Malcolm was normally attracted by – towards the rotting leaves.

Then, slowly – *very* slowly, like it was in super slo-mo – he saw Benny's head appear and start munching in that carefully-considering-every-morsel-of-manky-lettuce way tortoises eat; then Bjornita's head doing the same thing; and then he heard another voice say:

"Hey, Gav?"

"Yes, Mav?"

"Who's that?"

"Who's that who?"

"That tortoise?"

"It's Benny, isn't it?"

"No, Benny's here."

"Well, then it's Bjorn…"

"No, Bjorn's here too."

There was a long silence. Eventually, Malcolm heard Gavin say:

"So… there's a *third* tortoise?"

"Like… yuh! And yuh again!"

Another silence. Then:

"So… that means… that…"

"Yuh…?"

"Benny and Bjorn have had a *baby!* Hey! Great news!!"

At this point, Malcolm stuck his head out of the shell.

"No… look…" he said. "Gavin. Maven. I'm *not* a baby tortoise. I mean, I'm *obviously* not a baby tortoise. I'm too big for a start. Tortoises don't come out of the egg full-sized!"

Gavin and Maven looked at him. Gavin frowned. Maven frowned.[24]

"Anyway, never mind that," Malcolm continued. "Listen, I know this is hard to believe, but… I'm Malcolm Bailey! From the Bracket Wood Primary School trip! The boy who was standing at the back

---

[24] Obviously, these being humans, they were actually frowning.

when you were telling us about the goat! And I've been transformed… into a tortoise!!"

Gavin and Maven crouched down and stared at Malcolm closely. He looked up at them. *Thank God*, he thought, *they believe me; they* understand.

Then Gavin said:

"Wow. This one makes a lot of squeaky noises!"

CHAPTER FOURTEEN

That's porpoises

"Yuh!" said Maven. "Like babies do, I guess...
And hey! He's got blue eyes! Cute!"

"Yeah. Kind of unusual – for a tortoise. Anyway,"
said Gavin, getting up, "let's go and tell the kids
from Bracket Wood! And bring them out to see our
new baby tortoise! We can call it Benjorn!"

"Or Bjornny?"

"Or even Agnetha..."

"Fabulous idea! By the way, Gav, it's quite big

for a baby, isn't it?"

"Oh, they probably come out of the egg full-sized. Don't they?"

"Like, yuh!"

Malcolm heard their voices diminish. Through the hole in his shell, he could see their feet rushing away, tramping down the grass as they went.

"We can understand them," came a quieter voice from behind him. "But they can't understand us. Manky lettuce?"

Malcolm turned round. Benny was looking at him, his food laid out on the ground.

"No thanks," he said.

"Please yourself," said Benny, and tucked in. Bjornita was so busy eating she didn't even look up. Then Malcolm heard a host of excited children's voices.

"Where is it?"

"Where's the new baby tortoise?"

"Is he over here?"

Malcolm looked up. Rushing out of the farmhouse were all the Bracket Wood children and Mr Barrington.

Oh dear, thought Malcolm. *I really don't want to be surrounded by my year, all going on about what a lovely full-sized baby tortoise I am. I don't want to be picked up and stared at by Morris Fawcett. Or Fred and Ellie. Or Barry Bennett and his friends Jake, Lukas and Taj. Or Mr Barrington.*[25]

Malcolm shut his eyes. *Sleep,* he thought. *It might work. Benny might be right. In fact, he probably is – that is when I changed, when I fell asleep… OK, yes: that's definitely what's going to change me back to being a human. So come on: sleep.*

Of course, falling asleep isn't easy when you're *trying* to do it. It's fine when it's just something that happens. It's like falling off a log.[26] But when you're

---

[25] Interestingly, as a tortoise, Malcolm did somewhat resemble Mr Barrington. If Mr Barrington did pick him up and stare at him, all Malcolm really needed was a pair of tiny tortoise glasses for it to seem like Mr Barrington was looking in the mirror.

[26] This is something people say about stuff that's easy. However, please don't go to sleep when you're on a log. Especially one that's high up in a tree.

thinking about it – when you're lying there, with your mind going "Come on, got to go to sleep, I'm going to be really tired tomorrow otherwise" – it feels almost impossible.

So even though Malcolm, as we know, was really good at falling asleep, doing so at this particular moment – with thirty children, one teacher and two hipsters heading quickly towards him – felt very difficult. He heard them coming closer and closer.

"I love tortoises! They're like dolphins!"

"That's porpoises, Morris, you idiot!"

"Baby tortoise! Baby tortoise!"

"Benjorn!"

"Bjornny!"

Malcolm squeezed his eyes shut tighter, and then darted back into his shell.

Straight away it felt warm and safe again. And even though he could hear the voices of the children and Mr Barrington and Gavin and Maven

coming closer and closer, the safety of the shell had a massively calming effect on him, and he remembered just how good he was at falling asleep: and did.

CHAPTER FIFTEEN

Hello M

Mr Barrington was finding it very hard to see this so-called baby tortoise. Tortoises, he knew, had greeny-brown shells, and so would be difficult to pick out against this grass anyway, especially in the fading light. He was concerned that one of the children, all of whom had got overexcited and were running about madly, might step on it. He couldn't see very well, but he kept his ears cocked for a sickening crunch.

He didn't hear that noise, thankfully. What he did

hear was the sound of his phone ringing. *Lalalala,
lalalala, lalalala, laaa*.[27]

He reached inside his tweed jacket and took it out.

"Hello? Mr Barrington speaking?"

"Hello there, Mr Barrington. It's Malcolm Bailey's
mum, here – Jackie."

"Malcolm. Yes. Hello."

"I was just wondering if I could speak to him. See
how he's getting on."

Mr Barrington looked around. All of Year Six
appeared to be whirling round him. There were many
children, in a big, loud blur. *Oh heavens*, he thought,
not for the first time, *being a primary school teacher is not
an easy job for a man of my age*.

"Right. Yes. Of course. Er…" He reached out and
grabbed one of the boys. The boy looked up. Yes,
this one was Malcolm. Wasn't it?

---

[27] You know, that boring ringtone that grown-ups who don't know
how to download any other ones have.

"It's your mother on the line," said Mr Barrington.

In the Baileys' living room, Jackie said:

"Hello, M!"

"Oh. Hello, Mum," came the reply.

"How's it all going?" she said.

"Yeah, it's all right."

"Do you… like seeing the animals?"

"Yeah."

Although that didn't sound very convincing, Jackie's heart lifted. Maybe the school trip was having the desired effect?

"Oh, good! Have you learned anything?"

There was quite a long pause. So long, in fact, that Jackie thought the connection may have dropped out, and started looking at her phone. But then the voice came, saying the sentence quite slowly.

"Cows… don't… produce… *burgers.*"

Jackie took this in. "Right," she said. "Well. That's good, I'm sure."

"Yeah."

There was another pause. "Sorry, M, I can't hear you very well. Your voice sounds a bit strange, and there's a lot of shouting in the background."

"That's cos everyone's looking for a porpoise. No, wait a minute. Tortoise. Innit."

"Oh well," said Jackie, "it sounds fun. Although you sound a little... like you've got a cold or something. Are you keeping warm?"

"Don't fuss, Mum. Gotta go. See you soon!"

She heard a click, and the line went dead.

"How was that?" said Stewart, who was reading the newspaper on the other side of the room.

Jackie thought for a moment, then shrugged and said, "Better than I expected!"

CHAPTER SIXTEEN

Slurp slurp slurp

When Malcolm woke up, a little while later, he was sure he'd gone back to being a human. Because his vision was no longer full of grass and feet. His eyes were, clearly, operating at the right level. He had a great view, in fact, of his year group coming back towards the farmhouse, looking a bit disappointed.

"I don't know where it disappeared to," Gavin was saying. "When we went out to feed Benny and Bjorn, there was definitely another tortoise there!"

"Oh, there it is!" said Mr Barrington.

"No, Mr Barrington, that's just a big mound of manky lettuce," said Barry Bennett.

"Oh."

Very relieved, Malcolm assumed they'd spot him in a minute, and ask him where he'd been. *Wait till I tell them*, he thought. *Although they probably won't believe me!*

But strangely, all the children from his year – and Gavin and Maven, and Mr Barrington – just ignored him. They got closer and closer, without seeming to notice him at all. Then, weirdly, they seemed to pass *underneath* him.

At which point Malcolm realised his eyes weren't actually operating at the right level. He was higher up than everybody else.

He was, in fact, on the farmhouse roof.

Before he had a chance to consider how he might've got there, he heard someone scream:

"GETTᴛᴛᴛᴛOOFFFFFFFFFFMYYYYYYYROOOOOOOFFFF!!"

This was followed by a searing pain across his back. Malcolm jumped. *Really* jumped: much higher than he was expecting. As he reached the top of his jump, he looked down. Looking up at him, teeth bared, fur standing up, was the farm cat, Zsa-Zsa.

This was all very confusing. Why was he on the roof? How had he jumped so high? Why was the farm cat so angry with him?

Well, there was one obvious answer, which did occur to Malcolm, although he preferred not to think about it. But that was quite difficult, seeing as the other thing that was clueing him in as to what had happened was that his hands and feet, which he could see whirling around beneath him, were black, furry and clawed.

At least it meant that he landed gracefully.

"I SAID: GET OFF MY ROOF! THIS IS MY ROOF!

MY FARM! NO OTHER CATS ALLOWED!!"

"CALM DOWN!" said Malcolm. "I'M NOT A CAT!!"

"WHAT?"

"I'M NOT A CAT!!"

Zsa-Zsa looked at him. She looked and looked. Her eyes seemed to bore into him.

Then, very suddenly, she looked away and started washing herself.

Malcolm watched her, confused.

"So... you believe me?" said Malcolm. "We're good?"

"Of course I... *slurp slurp*... don't... *slurp*... believe you. I just noticed a speck of... *slurp*... dirt... on my shoulder."

"Right. So even though you're really angry, you thought you'd just stop the fight for a second to have a wash?"

Zsa-Zsa stopped licking herself and looked at him. "Yes. That's what we cats do. Don't pretend *you* don't!"

"I don't! Because I'm not a…" Unfortunately, just at that point, Malcolm spotted a tiny bit of matted fur on the side of his left front paw: and found himself unable, physically unable, not to bring his mouth towards it. It was like his tongue and teeth were made of iron and the bit of matted fur was a magnet. "…*slurp slurp*… cat."

"Oh, right…" said Zsa-Zsa. "I see. I see perfectly."

"I'm… *slurp slurp*…" Malcolm drew back his now slightly moist paw, and wiped it two or three times down the side of his face, "…*not!*"

Zsa-Zsa clearly didn't believe Malcolm. I say clearly, because she jumped on him, biting and scratching.

"DO YOU THINK I'M STUPID? DO YOU?!" she screamed at him. She was dragging his body round as she said this, in order to batter her back legs in his face.

"NO. OW! ALTHOUGH YOU ARE PURRING WHILE YOU'RE FIGHTING!! WHICH SEEMS A BIT STUPID!"

"CATS DO THAT TOO SOMETIMES!!"

"OH! RIGHT! OW!"

"DON'T PRETEND YOU DIDN'T KNOW!"

"OK, I DID KNOW—"

"AHA!" *Batter! Batter batter batter batter batter!* went her back legs. On his face.

"OWOWOWOWOW! BUT I ONLY KNOW BECAUSE I'VE HEARD OUR CATS DO IT! AT HOME! WHEN I WAS A HUMAN!!"

"THIS IS THE WORST LYING EXCUSE FOR ENCROACHING INTO ANOTHER CAT'S TERRITORY I'VE EVER HEARD!!"

"YOU CAN ASK THE TORTOISES!! BENNY AND BJORNITA!!"

This did actually make Zsa-Zsa stop battering him for a second. She rolled away, disdainfully.[28]

She stared at him, slightly more quizzically than before. Although still like she might jump on him at any moment. Or start washing. Which in fact she did. *Slurp. Slurp slurp*.

"So yes," said Malcolm, "you can ask the tor—"

"Shhh…" she said, her voice muffled by fur. "I'm thinking."

Slurp slurp slurp. Malcolm breathed heavily. He looked down at his feet. Which were not feet, really; they were paws. He noticed his claws were sharp. It occurred to him that he might, in fact, have been able to fight Zsa-Zsa off.

"OK," said Zsa-Zsa, stopping washing as suddenly

---

[28] This is quite hard to do, rolling disdainfully. Disdain is quite a hard emotion to get into a roll. But cats can do it. Cats can basically get disdain into every action.

as she started. "Something weird *is* going on here. Because only animals from this farm know about the transgender tortoise."

"She's not transgender. She's just a she. Who Gavin called Bjorn. She prefers Bjornita."

"Whatever. How do you *know* that?"

Malcolm sighed. What he was about to say seemed even less believable than that he was actually a human.

"Because I *was* a tortoise. Just now. Before I was a cat. I was speaking to the goat and—"

"OK, this is ridiculous," said Zsa-Zsa.

"I know!" said Malcolm. "But ask the tortoises!"

"I can't!" said Zsa-Zsa.

"Why not? They're just over there!" said Malcolm. In the middle distance, he could see Benny and Bjornita, like little tanks, circling the last pieces of manky lettuce.

"I don't speak tortoise."

"Oh."

This hadn't occurred to Malcolm. He'd assumed all animals could speak all other animals' languages. He, it seemed, could speak tortoise and cat. Although maybe he could only speak tortoise when he was a tortoise and cat when he was a cat. There was a lot to learn about being an animal.

"So…" said Malcolm, "how do you know about Bjorn wanting to be called Bjornita? If you don't speak tortoise?"

"I speak a bit of dog."

"Right…"

Malcolm looked at Zsa-Zsa for a while. She looked back at him, blankly.

"No, I don't understand how that helps," Malcolm said eventually.

Zsa-Zsa seemed to shake her head and tut, although she may have just been getting rid of a flea.

"The *dog* knows about the tortoises. He told me. Trotsky."

"Oh." Another short pause. "So Trotsky speaks tortoise?"

"No," said Zsa-Zsa. "He speaks frog. Which is pretty similar to tortoise. Apparently."

"Right."

"When he speaks it – the dog…"

"When the dog speaks frog," said Malcolm, thinking, *How am I saying these things? How can this actually be happening?*

"Yes – it's a kind of croak. I can't make it out at all. He just seems to be saying "sausages" over and over again. Anyway, I'll ask him."

"Ask him what?"

But before she could answer that, Zsa-Zsa – in three graceful leaps – had bounded down from the roof and was on the ground.

CHAPTER SEVENTEEN

Catamanny story

Malcolm watched from above, not sure whether to follow. Zsa-Zsa turned round and faced the doorway of the farm.

"Trotsky! Trotsky! Come here immediately!" she cried.

Within seconds, the farm sheepdog had appeared.

"Woof! Woof woof woof! Woof woof!"

OK, thought Malcolm. *Clearly, I don't understand dog.*

"Yes, yes. Whatever. Oy!" said Zsa-Zsa, looking up

at him. "What's your name?"

"Malcolm!"

"Malcolm? What kind of a name for a cat is that?"

"It's not a name for a cat. It's a name for a human. Cats aren't called things like that."

"Hmm. You say that, but I once heard the humans talking about a cat called – get this – *Dr. Seuss*. That's a cat who's a *doctor*! Not even a vet!"

Malcolm sighed. "That's the name of the author, not the cat," he said.

"What's an author?" said Zsa-Zsa.

"It's... never mind. Anyway, the Cat in the Hat isn't a real cat," he said.

Zsa-Zsa frowned. "Course it is. I saw a picture: furry, whiskers, tail, the lot."

"The big long hat didn't trouble you at all?"

"Nope. I assumed he was cold. Anyway, Malc—"

"Don't call me Malc!"

"I'll call you what I like. Malc – come down here!"

Malcolm looked down. *Directly* down. The ground suddenly seemed a long way off. He looked back to Zsa-Zsa. Trotsky the dog was with her, looking up at him, his tongue hanging expectantly out of his mouth.

"How do I do that?"

"Tsk! You're a cat!"

"No, I've told you, I'm a—"

"Look, even if your catamanny story about being a boy really is true – and I have to admit I haven't seen a cat with eyes that blue before – you're definitely rocking a cat's body right now. So I'm pretty sure that a hop on to the guttering, a shimmy down to the window, and a leap from there to here is going to be *no* problem."

Malcolm looked down again. It really looked high. Once, back when he had been a human boy – which was starting to feel like quite a long time ago – he had gone swimming with the school, and various boys had dared each other to dive from the top diving board at his local swimming pool. Barry, Lukas, Taj and Morris had all done it (although Morris had more fallen off than dived). But Malcolm couldn't: it looked not that high from the side of the pool, but once he'd walked up the ladder, right to the end of the board and looked down at the water, it felt like he was on top of a mountain. So, after trembling there for a bit, he just came down again, feeling sure that everyone in his year was looking at him and laughing.

This wasn't as high as that. Although proportionately it was, Malcolm thought, seeing as back then he had been four-and-a-half feet high, whereas now his head was about eight inches off the ground, or rather, the roof. So in terms of his present size, the drop was actually much, much higher.

So he just crouched there for a while, not knowing what to do and feeling scared. Then he heard Zsa-Zsa shout:

"Come on, Malc!"

"Pardon?" said Malcolm.

"I said come on, Malc! We haven't got all day!"

Two things got under Malcolm's fur about this.

1. He didn't like being called Malc.

2. Animals had nothing – nothing – to do. So the one thing they did have, as far as Malcolm could make out, was all day.

"Don't call me Malc!"

"Why not? It's short for Malcolm. All cats get their names shortened. Gav and Mav call me Zee-Zee."

"That isn't shorter!"

"Eh?"

"Zee-Zee takes as long to say as Zsa-Zsa!"

Zsa-Zsa yawned: this may or may not have been because she was bored. It was a cat yawn.

"Just come down, *Malc*!!"

Right, that's it, thought Malcolm. And in his anger, he just leapt into the air. For a moment, his paws whirled madly, as if he had no idea how to direct his flight.

But then suddenly, as if propelled by some internal steering wheel, his sleek cat body twirled towards the gutter, his back legs bouncing elegantly off it, directing him down towards the window ledge, where he landed for a split-second before bounding up again, and – by now thoroughly enjoying himself – spinning round in mid-air, twice, before settling, finally, on the grass exactly in between Trotsky and Zsa-Zsa.

Zsa-Zsa looked at him, wearily. "Yeah. Very un-catlike. I must say."

"That was fun!!" said Malcolm. "It was brilliant!"

"Modest too…" said Zsa-Zsa. "Oh, wait a minute," she added pointedly, her ears cocked. "What's that noise?"

"What noise?"

"*That* noise," said Zsa-Zsa.

Malcolm listened. He could hear a nice, comforting sound, a continuous breathy vibration, which sounded something like *phommm-pharrrr*…

"Where's that coming from?" he said.

"*You!* It's called *purring*, Mr I'm-Not-A-Cat! Anyway, Trotsky…?"

"Woof?"

"Can you ask the tortoises if this cat – Malcolm – was, just a minute ago, a tortoise?"

"Woof woof woof?"

"Yes, I know it's weird. Just ask them."

"Woof woof!"

"You won't look stupid. Or at least, no more stupid than you do when you sniff another dog's bum."

"Woof!"

"I do not. Well. Only if it's a cat I know really well."

Looking like he wasn't at all sure about that assertion, Trotsky turned round. So did Malcolm and Zsa-Zsa. Benny and Bjornita were approaching them. Slowly.[29]

Trotsky went off towards them.

Malcolm asked Zsa-Zsa: "How come Trotsky's just doing what you ask him? I thought dogs didn't like cats?"

Zsa-Zsa stared at him. "Now I'm starting to think you *might* be telling the truth about being a boy…"

"Why?"

"Because all real cats know that that whole *cats v dogs* thing is just an act. It's something we do for the humans: for their cartoons and stuff. In real life, we get on really well. Just as long as dogs know their place, of course."

"Woof woof woof!" said Trotsky. Zsa-Zsa and Malcolm turned round. Benny and Bjornita had finally got close enough.

---

[29] Would you believe it…

"OK, Trotsky, ask them! Ask them if *Malc* here was just one of them..."

"Woof!"

Trotsky crouched down. He sniffed at Benny. Then Bjornita. Malcolm watched, not entirely convinced the dog was going to talk to the tortoises. It looked more like he was about to eat them.

Then he went, in a low growl:

"Sausages sausages sausages. Sausages." His head whirled round, nodding towards Malcolm. "Sausages; sau-saaaaa-gesss." His head whirled back to the tortoises. "Sausages sausages sausages?"

"Yes," said Benny. "If that's Malcolm, he was just with us."

"And definitely, then, he looked like a tortoise," said Bjornita.

"Oh!" said Malcolm. "I can understand you two! Maybe... then... I can understand the languages of animals I've... been...?"

"Sorry," said Zsa-Zsa, "now it sounds like *you're* just saying 'sausages'..."

"I can talk to the tortoises! Hi, Benny! Hi, Bjornita!"

"Hello, Malc!" said Benny.

"Don't call me Malc!"

"I understand that," said Bjornita. "Malc-olm. How's life as a cat now?"

"It's great!"

"I see. Better than being a tortoise?"

"Er..."

Bjornita turned away, haughtily. "Well, I think your silence speaks volumes. Doesn't it, Benny?"

"What do you mean, Bjornita?"

"I mean, *clearly*, he thinks it's better being a cat than a tortoise..."

"Well," said Benny, "it probably is."

"Don't say that."

"Sorry. But sometimes I think I'd quite like *fur*. And *speed*. And people stroking me. And lots of photos of me looking cute on the internet."

"Hello?" said Zsa-Zsa. "I have no idea what you chaps are saying to each other. But I *am* still here. And I am still waiting for an answer to the question: was this cat very recently a tortoise?"

"Woof woof woof!" said Trotsky.

"Oh, use your cat words, Trotsky," said Zsa-Zsa.

"Woof… woof woof…?" he said quietly.

"Don't be silly. Your accent isn't stupid."

Trotsky raised his eyes, looking a bit ashamed.[30] Then he said:

"Yeeeesss. Zeee Tortoize lady-one and not lady-one, zeey sayy zat zey are thinking zat zis kitty is yes Malcolm the boy-human who was also just now a tortoise yes."

---

[30] Obviously, being a dog, Trotsky could really do this.

Zsa-Zsa looked at Malcolm. "Blimey…" she said.

"You see!" said Malcolm, feeling vindicated at last.

"…I'd forgotten quite how stupid his accent in fact is."

CHAPTER EIGHTEEN

So cat

"OK," said Zsa-Zsa, "so… you're a boy."

"Yes," said Malcolm.

"And… now you're a cat."

"Yes."

"So… what's the problem?"

"Pardon?"

Zsa-Zsa scratched her ear with her back foot, quite hard, like she was banging her head against her toes. Then said: "Well, that's an improvement. Isn't it?"

"Er… well. I don't know."

"You're prettier. You're cleverer. You get to sleep twenty-three hours a day."

"And poo outdoors…" said Benny.

"Yes, that too. What's not to love? About being a cat."

Malcolm was about to say, "No! You don't understand! I don't even *like* animals! So can you imagine what it's like suddenly being one?" but stopped himself.

Not *just* because that might have sounded rude. But because for a minute – for a second – he thought: *Actually, she might have a point.* He felt how taut and streamlined his body was. He remembered that jump down from the roof. He realised that he was, in a way, having *fun*.

So instead he said:

"Well. Not everything's great about being a cat."

"Name one thing that isn't," said Zsa-Zsa.

Malcolm thought about something Ticky and Tacky did at home. Weirdly, it gave him a bit of a pang, thinking about home and his own family's cats. Even if he didn't like them.

"Well," he said, "have you by any chance found, inside the farmhouse, a lovely small pond – surrounded by white slopes?"

"Oh yes!" said Zsa-Zsa. "It's in the room where Gavin and Maven bathe."

Malcolm smiled to himself. "And do you sometimes balance yourself on those slopes and then bend your face right down to drink water from that lovely pond?"

"Yes?" said Zsa-Zsa.

"It's a toilet. It's a human toilet."

Zsa-Zsa didn't say anything for a moment. "Hmm. I thought the water tasted... a bit... *tangy*..." She licked herself. "Oh well."

Obviously not even making it clear that she'd drunk gallons of toilet water was going to dent Zsa-Zsa's love of being a cat. So Malcolm said:

"Anyway. I think what I should do – at least to try and find out what's happened – is go and speak to K-Pax."

"The goat?"

"Yes."

"What's he got to do with it?"

Malcolm realised he hadn't actually explained to Zsa-Zsa how he'd ended up like this. So he did.

"Hmm," said Zsa-Zsa after he'd finished. "Sounds a bit... far-fetched..."

"Well..." said Malcolm. "Yes."

"Oh, that's so typical," said Bjornita. "So cat!"

"What did the tortoise say?" said Zsa-Zsa.

"Um," said Malcolm.

"Spit it out."

"She, er, said, 'That's so typical. So *cat*.'"

Zsa-Zsa narrowed her eyes at Bjornita.[31]

"I beg your pardon?"

"You being so cynical and disbelieving about it!" said Bjornita. "That's very cat."

Zsa-Zsa looked at Malcolm. Reluctantly, Malcolm translated.

"Oh right," said Zsa-Zsa, "as opposed to being all –" she went close to Bjornita and screwed up her face to look stupid – "*durrrrrghgghhh* about it. That's very *tortoise*. Translate, please, Malcolm."

Malcolm chose not to do this. Instead he said, "Listen. I think we're getting away from the problem. Which is, um, *my* problem, mainly. Because I would like to get back to being a boy, at some point." He took a deep breath, trying to control the fear that saying this brought up in him. "So. Does anyone speak goat?"

---

[31] This is something cats can do. I've seen it. It's quite frightening.

Trotsky and Benny and Bjornita and Zsa-Zsa shook their heads.

"OK…" said Malcolm. "But I've got an idea anyway. Let's go to the goat pen…"

"Why?" said Benny.

"I think," said Malcolm, "that the way this works is… when I fall asleep, I *change*. Into another animal! I think… into the last animal I saw. That's what happened just now – I saw Zsa-Zsa on the roof just before I went to sleep and when I woke up I was a cat. So… if I get into the goat pen, I could fall asleep. And then I'll wake up as a goat! And then I could speak to K-Pax."

There was a short pause while the other animals took in this quite long speech. Then Bjornita said:

"Splendid idea!"

"Good one!" said Benny.

"Meee thinking it soundzzzz goooood," said Trotksy. "Yezzz. Goooood."

"OK," said Zsa-Zsa. "Let's go!"

"Yeah," said Benny. "Let's go!"

"What did he say?" said Zsa-Zsa, as she ran off, followed closely by Trotsky and Malcolm.

"Never mind," said Malcolm, looking back at Benny and Bjornita, already a long way behind.

CHAPTER NINETEEN

Hey, boy

When they got to the goat pen, Zsa-Zsa jumped gracefully up and sat on the edge of the fence. Malcolm followed her. It was so easy to land there – it was amazing. Trotsky made more of a meal of it, scrabbling up with his tongue hanging out, and then he wasn't able to perch on the fence, so just fell off on to the earth on the other side, which made most of the goats back away.

Malcolm looked at Trotsky, and felt... superior.

Which was odd. When he was a boy he wouldn't have felt that a cat was better than a dog or any other animal. He wouldn't have cared either way. But as a cat, he definitely felt he was better than a dog. Or any other animal.

"So," said Zsa-Zsa, "which one is K-Pax?"

Malcolm looked at the goats, still all backing away from Trotsky, who was just wagging his tail at them. Then, behind all the others, he saw: those eyes, those amber, staring eyes.

"That one," he said. "The really old-looking one at the back."

"OK. Well, go to sleep."

"Right… just like that."

"Well, if you're right, you'll turn into a goat. Then you can talk to K-Pax."

"Yes…" Malcolm was suddenly a bit frightened about this. He had felt, at some level, quite at home with being a cat. Being a goat: that seemed more alien.

Then again, he had already been a tortoise.

So he jumped down into the pen. The ground was muddy, covered in hay and straw. The goats were all staring at him. It didn't feel like the easiest place to sleep, even if he was a cat, the best animal at sleeping in the world.

But then Trotsky came over and said:

"Perhapzzzz zis will help???"

He curled his body round Malcolm, like a warm, furry, all-over body-pillow. And within seconds, Malcolm felt himself falling asleep.

Just before Malcolm actually dropped off, however, he heard the gate of the goat pen open.

And some voices.

"Gav!"

"Yes, Mav?"

"They'll be all right in here, won't they? Then

they'll be in place already for the show tomorrow morning…"

"Yuh! Oh look, here's Trotsky!"

"Cuddling some cat."

"Who is that cat?"

"Don't know. Looks really like Zsa-Zsa. But she's back at the farmhouse, eating. Hey, Trot! Hey, boy! Where have you been? We needed you to help move all the sh—"

But by then Malcolm was asleep.

CHAPTER TWENTY

The Dollys

"WAKE UP! WAKE UP, EVERYBODY! IT'S TIME TO WAKE UP! HOW MANY TIMES DO I HAVE TO SAY IT?! WAKEY-WAKEY!!"

Malcolm did as he was told. He woke up.

The person speaking was:

– shouting very, very loudly and repeatedly in front of him

– and also, a cockerel.

"Urggh…" said Malcolm, blinking. "How come I

can speak cockerel?"

"EVERY ANIMAL SPEAKS COCKEREL! WE ALL HAVE TO! BECAUSE WE ALL HAVE TO KNOW WHAT TIME TO GET UP! IT'S VITAL!!" The cockerel stuck his face closer to Malcolm's. "WAAAAAAAKKKKKKEEEEEE-UPPPPPPPP!!"

Malcolm looked at the cockerel, who was puffing his chest out and shaking his weird gibbly under-chin bits and his red punk washing-up-glove hairdo with the effort of telling Malcolm to wake up.

"I'm awake," said Malcolm, deadpan.

The cockerel looked at him, suspiciously.

"Hmm. OK," he said, and turned away. "WAKE UP!!"

"No one else in here is asleep!" said a voice.

"Certainly not any more!" said another voice.

"GOOD! WAKE UP!!"

Malcolm looked up at the sky. It was a new day – a nice day: the sun was shining and the sky, visible above the fence of the goat pen, was blue. He felt refreshed by his sleep. And the plan had clearly worked. He looked down at his feet, which were hooved. He scratched his head on the floor and could feel that he had little horns. And the smell rising from him was very – well, it was very Stinky Blinky.

He looked around for K-Pax. Yes. He was still there, in the same place, behind a couple of other goats.

Great, thought Malcolm. *I can get him to reverse the spell and then I'll be a boy again.*

Malcolm walked – trotted – over towards that area of the pen. He wondered how to approach this. At first he thought perhaps he would just speak to K-Pax gently, in order to coax out of him the way back to being human.

But as the other goats parted, and he got closer and closer, he became angrier. If indeed this whole thing *was* K-Pax's doing, what right did the old goat have to change him into a variety of different animals? It wasn't fair to inflict that on someone else! Just because Malcolm had said he didn't like animals! Never mind being gentle! Malcolm was going to tell him off! As his grandpa liked to say, he was going to give him what for!

Finally, he had the goat in his sights. K-Pax was right in front of him. Malcolm saw once again the staring amber eyes that had, he was sure now, caused this whole animal thing.

Malcolm opened his mouth and said, loudly:

"Baa! Baa-baa-baa-baa *baaaaa*-baaa. BAA-BAA!" Then a short pause. And then: "Baaa?"

I mean, Malcolm *thought* he was saying:

"Oy! Look here, K-Pax, or whatever your name is! What do you think you're doing turning boys into animals!! Eh?"

But if you'd been a human, and there at the time, you'd definitely have heard:

"Baa! Baa-baa-baa-baa *baaaaa*-baaa. BAA-BAA!" And then: "Baaa?"

Which might explain why K-Pax just stared at him. And also why Malcolm was suddenly surrounded by three sheep.

"Hello!"

"Hello!"

"Hello!"

they said.

"Sorry, what's going on?" said Malcolm.

"That's what we were wondering," said the first one. "Why are you shouting at that goat? He doesn't understand sheep."

"He doesn't! Not sheep!" said the second one.

"Not a word of sheep! *Baa-baa-baa* is all he hears!" said the third one.

Malcolm shut his eyes and took a deep breath. "So. You're telling me that… I'm a sheep?" he said, with his eyes closed.

"YES!" they all said together.

"What's your name?" said Sheep 1.

Malcolm opened his eyes.

"Malcolm. What's yours?"

"Dolly!" replied Sheep 1.[32]

"I'm also Dolly!"

"I'm Dolly too!"

"Right… sorry, I thought this was the *goat* pen?"

"It is," said Dolly 1. "But our field's being dug up. So Gavin and Maven put us in here for the night."

"Hmm. When they led you in here, did you notice a sleeping cat… not Zsa-Zsa – another one?"

"No."

"No."

"Yes!"

Dolly 1 and Dolly 2 looked at Dolly 3.

"That's odd," said Dolly 1.

"Yes," said Dolly 2. "We always agree with each other. Usually."

---

[32] Who from now on I shall call Dolly 1. Sheep 2 will be Dolly 2. And Sheep… you get the picture.

"Yes," replied Dolly 1. "I agree with *you*, and you agree with *me*, and *we* agree with *her*."

"Yes!" said Dolly 3. "I agree with you! I *do* normally agree with you!"

"Agreed!" said Dolly 1, 2 and 3.

Malcolm closed his eyes again. He thought he could feel a headache coming on. He tried to rub his head with his hand. But then he remembered that he didn't have a hand, he had a hoof. And that it was very difficult for a sheep to raise a single hoof to its head for a rub.[33]

"So…" said Dolly 3, "I know this is weird…"

"Weird," said Dolly 2.

"Yes, weird," said Dolly 1.

"But even though you two *didn't* see the cat… I did?"

This seemed to completely stump Dolly 1 and Dolly 2. Even, in fact, Dolly 3. Who was saying it.

---

[33] And even if he did manage it, Malcolm's hoof was so hard, he might knock himself out. He thought.

So she added:

"Maybe… I imagined it?"

"Yes, I agree," said Dolly 1.

"So do I," said Dolly 2.

"And me!" said Dolly 3, sounding *very* relieved.

"Anyway!" said Malcolm. "Do any of you speak *goat?*"

They all shook their heads.

"Isn't it very similar to sheep?" said Malcolm. "I mean it sounds quite similar. Like… I dunno…" A very faint memory came back to him, of something they had learned in school. "Spanish and Italian?"

"No, no," said Dolly 1. "We *baa*. Goats *bray*."

"Baa!" said Dolly 2.

"Not bray!" said Dolly 3.

"Right," said Malcolm. "Got it. Thanks. But can't you – can't *we* – *try*, though?"

"No."

"Don't think so."

"Not possible."

said the three sheep.

Hmm, thought Malcolm, suddenly having an idea.

"Really?" he said. "Even though *I'd* like to do it? And I'm a sheep, and sheep always agree with each other…"

The Dollys looked at each other.

"OK!" they said, in unison.

CHAPTER TWENTY-ONE

Goaty McGoatface

So the four sheep began to trot over together to confront K-Pax. Who seemed to be waiting for them, in exactly the same place as before.

Suddenly the way to the old goat was blocked by a ring of other goats, who surrounded him like armed guards.

"Stop, sheep!" said one of the goats, in a very big important voice. "Go no further."

"Oh, goat and sheep *is* quite similar then…" said Dolly 1.

"Yes, more similar than I realised!" said Dolly 2.

"Almost *exactly* the same…" said Dolly 3.

"Hello," said Malcolm. "What is your name?"

"Goaty McGoatface," said the goat.

"Really?" said Malcolm.

"Yes. It is apparently a very dignified and proper name for a goat, according to Gavin and Maven."

Malcolm did his best not to laugh, which actually wasn't that difficult, as sheep can't.

"What is your purpose with K-Pax?" said Goaty McGoatface, in an even bigger and more important voice.

"I just want to know why he changed me into an animal!" said Malcolm.

The circle of goats closed tighter round K-Pax, muttering to each other in small noises that Malcolm couldn't understand, possibly because they were speaking in a goaty dialect that wasn't very sheepy.

Then Goaty McGoatface said (big, important, etc.):

"K-Pax does not speak!"

"Yes, I do!" said a voice from inside the circle of goats. It was quite an old man's voice, a little bit like Grandpa Theo's. Only with a bit of a goaty vibrato in it.

"What was that?" said Malcolm.

"Nothing," said Goaty McGoatface.

"Nothing!"

"Nothing!"

"Nothing!"

...said the other goats in the circle.

"As I was saying," Goaty continued, "K-Pax is the great, silent goat. His wisdom is that of the ancients, and cannot be passed on by words..."

"No, it's OK!" said the voice again. "I'm up for a chat!"

Malcolm stared at Goaty.

"That was K-Pax!" he said.

"No, it wasn't!"

"It wasn't!"

"It wasn't!"

"Yes, it was me! Hello, Malcolm!" said the voice. It was muffled, coming as it did from behind the tight circle of goats.

"Hello, K-Pax! Why won't your goat friends let me talk to you?" said Malcolm, loudly, trying to raise his head above the goats (which wasn't easy as they had horns as well).

"I know," said K-Pax, trying to peer through the ring of goats surrounding him. "It's annoying. They think it makes me more mysterious and

magical and stuff if I don't speak."

"Can you hear something?" said Goaty McGoatface, bigly, importantly.

"No," said another goat. "Well, I can hear the sheep speaking. Apart from that, nothing."

"Why do they want you to be more mysterious?" said Malcolm.

"I dunno. Not a lot happens in this goat pen, to be honest. So when something magical does go on they like to make it as glamorous as possible. Anyway, how's it going?"

"What?"

"Being an animal. How are you finding it?"

How am I finding it…? thought Malcolm. Like K-Pax was asking him about having a new pair of shoes! Or being in a different class at school!

"Oh, it's fine," said Malcolm, sarcastically. "Super."

Unfortunately, animals – well, except for cats, obviously – do not understand sarcasm.

"Oh good," said K-Pax. "I *knew* it was what you wanted, from what you said! To understand animals, you have to live as an animal!"

"No," said Malcolm, "wait a minute…"

"Just remember," K-Pax continued, with some deepness in his voice, "when the cockerel has crowed three times, the spell will be over!"

"When the cockerel has crowed three times?" said Malcolm. "Do you mean… after three days?"

"Um… yes. Suppose so. I think it sounds better to say 'when the cockerel has crowed three times', though – sounds more… y'know… *spell*-ish…"

"Oh good!" said Malcolm. "So I'll be a boy again in three days?"

Well, he thought, *that's not too bad*.

"No…" said K-Pax. "When the cockerel has crowed three times, you will transform into whatever animal you wake up with that morning. So on the third night, time's up: you have to decide which animal you want to be. Then all you have to do is get close to that animal and go to sleep near it: and when you wake up, you'll be that one *forever!* That's how you'll become what you're meant to be! Oh, I knew you'd come to love animals once you were one!"

If Malcolm had still been a boy his face would've turned white. Being as he was a sheep, it just was white. But inside, it turned whiter.

"Only make sure that it's an animal you really like," K-Pax was continuing. "An animal you love, preferably, and who loves you!"

"Sorry…" said Malcolm, "did you say… forever?"

"WAKEY-WAKEY!!"

Malcolm turned away from the goat throng. The cockerel was passing by the outside of the goat pen, still on a mission to destroy sleep on Orwell Farm.

Which made something very clear to Malcolm.

Horribly clear.

"But… I've already had one day. And night!"

"OK!" said K-Pax. "Two days left! So get weaving!"

"Weaving?"

"With those animal choices! Gotta make sure you choose the right one!"

Malcolm gulped. "It is reversible?"

"Is what reversible?"

"The spell! The being-an-animal thing!"

"Why would you want that?" said K-Pax, still from behind a wall of other goats, who were all looking around, pretending they couldn't hear him.

"Because I don't *want* to be an animal. I never wanted to be an animal! I want to be a boy again!"

Suddenly K-Pax did, actually, fall silent.

"K-Pax?"

"The Great Lord K-Pax, as I have told you, sheep, does not speak!" intoned Goaty McGoatface.

"That just isn't true, is it, Goaty? I was just speaking to him."

"No, you weren't!" said K-Pax.

"That's him now!" said Malcolm. "Saying I wasn't!"

"Well then," said Goaty, "clearly you weren't."

"What? How can I not have been speaking to him when he just spoke to me to tell me I wasn't speaking to him! It doesn't make any sense!"

"And neither, my friend, do you! Now, if you wouldn't mind backing AWAY from the goat – nothing to see here…"

Malcolm had a feeling he knew what had happened; why K-Pax wasn't speaking to him. Because when Malcolm asked if the spell was reversible, it was clear that Malcolm *hadn't* really wanted to be an animal at all, and K-Pax didn't want to admit to having made a mistake.

None of which was going to help Malcolm to become a boy again.

OK, thought Malcolm. *These goats clearly won't listen to reason. Time to use brute force. And the fact that sheep always do what other sheep do.*

"Dollys!" he said, turning to them. "Follow me!"

"OK!"

"OK!"

"OK!"

Malcolm put his head down, ready to charge the goats. Each of the Dollys did the same. Goaty McGoatface tensed. There was a distant squeal that may or may not have been K-Pax.

Then suddenly the door opened and four large men Malcolm had never seen before, wearing aprons, came into the pen. Round their chests were straps, leading to long leather bags, from which Malcolm could see poking out what looked like very long and sharp… *knives*.

"Get the sheep!!" shouted one of the men.

Dollys 1, 2 and 3 stopped facing the goats, and just turned and ran.

So did Malcolm, who suddenly found he *really* wanted to do what the other sheep did.

CHAPTER TWENTY-TWO

Blades at the ready

But it was too late! Malcolm saw Dolly 1, Dolly 2 and Dolly 3 caught by the men!

It looked very rough: three of the men grabbed the sheep by their back legs, and swung them upside down. And before he knew it, the fourth man – a very large man indeed – had got *Malcolm's* legs, and swung *him* upside down! And yes, it *was* very rough!

The man carried him over his shoulder to the other side of the pen. Malcolm could see the points of his various knives, glinting in the no-longer-nice-at-all sunlight.

"Help!" shouted Malcolm. "Help! Help!"

"Yes!" shouted Dolly 1. "Help!"

"Help!" shouted Dolly 2.

"Help help help!" shouted Dolly 3.

"Hi!" said Gavin, suddenly coming into the pen.

"Hi!" said Maven, also suddenly coming into the pen.

"Oh, thank heavens!" said Malcolm. "Gavin! Maven! They'll stop all this!"

"'Allo there, sir and madam," said the man who was carrying Malcolm. "Sorry the sheep be making so much noise today!"

"No worries," said Gavin. "No need to call us sir and madam, though, Eli!"

"Right you are, sir and madam."

"Everything sorted?" said Maven.

"Blades at the ready?" said Gavin.

"Yes, sir and madam!" said the man called Eli.

"Oh no!" shouted Malcolm. "Gavin! Maven! Please!"

"Mr Barrington?" said Gavin.

"We're here!" Malcolm heard Mr Barrington's voice.

What?

"Everybody! Children! This way!"

Malcolm felt himself swung back over the man's shoulder and on to the ground. The man was holding him down. It hurt. He could see the same thing was happening to the Dollys.

Meanwhile, along the top edge of the fence, he could suddenly also see the faces of: Fred, Ellie, Barry, Lukas, Jake, Taj, Isla, Morris and all the rest of his year.

Mr Barrington raised a hand for silence. "OK, all of you. Gavin and Maven have very kindly organised today's event. So watch closely…"

"Mr Barrington?"

"Yes, Ellie?"

"Should we watch closely where the sheep are? Or the way you're facing?"

"Oh. Sorry. I see now that those are just some fluffy clouds. No, look over here!"

They all turned to look into the pen.

Of *course*, thought Malcolm. *We're here, on a farm. And what happens on a farm? What happens to the animals? I can't believe it. I can't believe it's going to end this way! With all my year watching!*

He looked up and screamed:

"Barry! Fred! Ellie! Lukas! Mr Barrington, sir! I'm not a sheep! I don't want to be chops! Or stew! Save me! Save me!"

"Haha! Baa! Baa!" said Morris. "That sheep is going baa at us!"

"Yes," said Isla with a sigh. "That's what they do."

Oh no, thought Malcolm. It was no good. He was just doing a lot of mad baa-ing. It was pointless. Malcolm felt very, very sad; he closed his eyes.

Then, with his free hand – the one that wasn't holding Malcolm down – the man called Eli reached into his leather bag.

CHAPTER TWENTY-THREE

Run run run!

Malcolm's eyes were still closed – he may have closed them tighter – when he heard a strange noise. Sort of like a very, very buzzy fly. He wondered if maybe, to save his life, he'd had a last-minute transformation – into a very, very buzzy fly.

But then he opened his eyes, and saw his hooves, and Mr Barrington squinting at him, and realised that, no: he was still a sheep.

He wasn't, though, dead. What he *was*, was a bit

colder around the bottom area than he had been before. And also, wanting to laugh. Because he was being *tickled*. *Around* the bottom area.

"Ha-ha-ha-ha!! Ha! Stop it! Stop it!!" he said.

"Shush!" said Eli. "God. This one's acting like he's never been sheared before!"

Malcolm looked round. Using electric shears, Eli was shaving off the wool on his back. Every so often, where there were knots, Eli would cut them off with a knife, from the leather bag.

Malcolm tried to stop laughing, but not only did it tickle, it felt completely silly that huge clods of wool were coming off him: it was like he was a very cosy version of Spider-Man, whose body produced not steel-like threads of silk for enmeshing supervillains, but balls for grannies to knit with. And then, to make it worse, Eli turned Malcolm over, and started to do his tummy.

"That one's got a funny *Baaa!*" he heard Barry

Bennett say, above his own laughing.

"Yes," said his friend Lukas. "It sounds more like *Baa-Ha-Ha* than *Baaaa!*"

Finally, it was over, and Eli let him go. Malcolm and the Dollys stood up among their shorn wool. It looked like the goat pen had been overlaid with a very badly made shagpile carpet.

"So there you are, boys and girls," said Gavin. "That's how you shear a sheep!"

There was a round of applause. Which felt odd to Malcolm. He had never thought about applauding his dad after watching him shave.

"Ah, that's better!" said Dolly 1.

"Yes, much better!" said Dolly 2.

"Better all round!" said Dolly 3.

"I think it's cold and a bit embarrassing," said Malcolm.

"Yes, that's right, cold and embarrassing," said Dolly 1.

"Embarrassing and cold," said Dolly 2.

"Freezing!" said Dolly 3. "And quite humiliating."

"Also," said Malcolm, "why were you shouting 'help' earlier? You must have known it was only a shearing?"

The Dollys looked at him blankly.

"We were shouting help because *you* were shouting help," said Dolly 1.

"Yes, because *you* were—"

"Yes, all right," said Malcolm, sighing. "I get it."

"Now," said Maven, "let's take the sheep back to their field!"

Suddenly, over the goat-pen fence bounded Trotsky. As soon as they saw the dog, Dolly 1, Dolly 2 and Dolly 3 ran towards the gate, which was

opened by Eli. Then they carried on running. Malcolm watched them go. He was starting to have had enough of the whole sheep thing.

"That's odd," said Eli. "That one sheep don't seem very bothered by the dog."

"Woof woof woof!" said Trotsky, nudging at Malcolm's back. Malcolm shook his head.

"OK, children," said Gavin, "perhaps you can help us get this sheep out of here!"

Next thing Malcolm knew, he was surrounded by his own classmates, cheering and whooping and going: "Come on, sheepy!", "Wake up, lambkin!" and "Where's your wool-coat gone? Where's your wool-coat gone?"

So just to get away from them – Morris Fawcett was being particularly annoying, poking him on his newly-shorn rump – Malcolm ran out of the goat pen and after the Dollys.

And then his year ran out of the goat pen and chased him.

After a few minutes, Barry and Lukas and Taj and Fred and Ellie had caught up with Malcolm. They were all laughing and joking and giggling as they ran. It made Malcolm feel envious, and a bit sad, that they were having such a lot of fun and he wasn't. He was just running.

"Barry!" said Malcolm, while still running. "Lukas! Taj! Fred! Ellie! It's me! Malcolm!"

"This one's really funny!" said Lukas. "He just keeps baa-ing as he runs!"

"Yes, and he's looking right at us!" said Fred. "Like he's actually trying to tell us something!"

"I am trying to tell you something!" said Malcolm.

"Baa-baa! Baa-baa!" said Taj, imitating him. Which made them all laugh. And then they ran off back towards the farmhouse, leaving the sheep far behind.

Malcolm carried on running, and caught up with the Dollys. He trotted along with them, in the middle of a big field.

"Where are we going?" he said.

"We're running away!" said Dolly 1.

"Away! Running!" said Dolly 2.

"Far far far!" said Dolly 3.

"But… the kids chasing us… they caught up with us already. Now, in fact, they're just running in front of us! Look! There's Barry and Lukas and Taj and Fred and Ellie and all the rest of them, about fifty metres ahead!"

"We have to run!" said Dolly 1.

"Run run run!" said Dolly 2.

"But it looks like *we're* chasing *them* now!"

"Keep going!" said Dolly 3. "They might catch up!"

"They *have* caught up!"

"Onward!" said Dolly 1.

It was at that point that Malcolm stopped *starting*
to have had enough with the whole sheep thing.

He *finished* having had enough with the whole
sheep thing. He stopped, let the Dollys run on, and
just settled down in the field, to go to sleep.

CHAPTER TWENTY-FOUR
Brill poo

"Mr Braden?" said Jackie, opening the door from the reception area to the surgery. "Rodney?"

"What is it? I'm examining a gerbil."

"I know…"

"It's got a very unusual condition. Only by extreme focus and concentration can I restore it to health."

"I thought he'd eaten a crayon," said Jackie. "A purple one."

"It has."

"Is that… an unusual condition?"

"If I show you the X-rays, Jackie you'll see that…"

His insides have gone purple? His tiny gerbil bladder actually has a drawing on it of a purple house and some purple clouds? was what Jackie Bailey was thinking.

But she didn't say it, as Rodney Braden the vet was her boss, and someone who took his veterinary work very, very seriously. So she just let him waffle on about how the X-rays showed some toxic effects on the gerbil's tummy – obviously he didn't say tummy, he said intestines – until finally he took a breath.

"Yes, of course, Rodney, I realise you're very busy doing extremely delicate work with Gandhi…"

"Who's Gandhi?"

"The gerbil."

Rodney looked down at the tiny creature anaesthetised in front of him, as if surprised that, beyond being a collection of organs, it had a name.

"I know him," continued Jackie. "He's Jinesh's – Mr and Mrs Bhaskar's son's gerbil. They live two doors down from us."

"Right. Well, as I say, Jackie, I'm very busy… the operation is at an absolutely crucial stage…"

"Yes. I was just wondering if I could use the landline to make a personal call. To my son – at this farm, this school trip he's on. My mobile's run out of power."

Of course, if you weren't so mean, she thought, *I wouldn't have had to come in and ask that.*

She watched the vet frown, caught, she knew, between two opposing instincts:

1. Wanting to say no, as it cost money.
2. Wanting to say yes, whatever, just go away, so that he could carry on being the great and serious vet.

At that point, while the vet was frowning, Ghandi's tiny body twitched. It might just have been a purple crayon-y burp, but it was enough to make up Rodney Braden's mind.

"Yes, whatever!" he said, waving her away.

Gavin was just cutting the Stinky Blinky when the farmhouse phone rang. Which might explain why no one heard it at first, as almost everyone in the room was going "*uuurggh*" and "*arrrgghh*" and "my eyes are watering!"

But Maven, who was smiling and licking her lips, picked it up.

"Hi!" said Maven.

"Hello? Sorry, I was going to call Mr Barrington's mobile, but the reception wasn't very good last time, so I thought I'd call the farmhouse landline… anyway, sorry, it's Jackie Bailey, Malcolm's mother."

"Cool."

Jackie wasn't quite sure what to say to that. So she said:

"Yes. Thanks. Um. Anyway, is Malcolm there?"

"Wait a minute…" said Maven. "Uh… Gavin?"

"Hey, Maven," said Gavin, handing her a plate. "The Blinky's just *so* stinky tonight. You *gotta* try it."

"OK!" Maven took a large slice and held it in front of her mouth.

"Sorry, hello?" said Jackie. "I was wondering about Malcolm?"

"Oh yuh. Soz."

She put the phone down and addressed the dining room.

"Is Malcolm here? Malcolm Bailey?"

Well, that's what Maven was trying to say. Unfortunately, she chose to put the big piece of Stinky Blinky in her mouth first. And so it came out as:

"Ibrgh Molkolmmm blah? Mollkollloommm Bladibley?"

Which very few of the children heard above their own shouts of "urggh", "arrrgh" and now also "I'm going to be sick!"

"Soz," said Maven. "Oy dink hee mblguht pee sglight oootgird pleepggin wlgh de anishckmals."

"I beg your pardon?" said Jackie.

Maven did a big – and to be honest, even though she always said how much she liked it, quite forced (she closed her eyes and screwed up her face, anyway) – swallow. "Oh blimey," she said, taking a long breath. "Soz again. I said: I think he might be still outside playing with the animals."

Which was at least true.

At that point, at the vet's, Rodney reappeared. He came out of the surgery, holding Gandhi the gerbil in one hand, and a half-digested purple crayon in the other. Despite the obvious success of the operation, he – Rodney – was looking cross (Ghandi, to be honest, was looking just a bit bemused).

Jackie knew why this was: she'd been on the phone too long.

"OK, well… send him my love when he comes in!" said Jackie, hurriedly putting the phone down. So hurriedly, in fact, she didn't hear Maven say, "Brill poo!"

Which was her way of saying "Will do!"

…with her mouth full of more Stinky Blinky.

CHAPTER TWENTY-FIVE

A lovely name

Malcolm had been hoping, on waking, to be a horse. That was his plan. As he had been running across the field with the sheep, he'd noticed a group of horses in the next field. That was why, apart from having had enough of being a sheep, he'd chosen that spot to go to sleep in.

He wanted to be a horse not just because he thought being a horse might be great – proud and dignified and strong and fast and not-sheep-like –

but also because he had had an idea.

If he was a horse, he could get back home. He didn't exactly know the way, and he didn't exactly know, when he got there, how he was going to communicate to his mum and dad that he was not just any old horse come off the street and into their house, but was, in fact, their son Malcolm. He decided, however, not to worry about that just yet.

He was sure that, somehow, Stewart and Jackie would recognise him, and sort everything out. They didn't, it was true, have a lot of practical experience with goat spells. But they were his mum and dad. And they would know what to do. He hoped.

On waking, though, he was also fairly sure that, once again, he hadn't ended up as the animal he'd planned. Because he wasn't cantering majestically through the fields, tossing his mane in the wind.

No. Rather, he was lying face-down in some mud. He seemed to actually be breathing in mud. He tried to get up, but just slipped, and sank further into the mud. He looked up. The sun was significantly lower in the sky than it had been when he went to sleep. The day was slipping away and he'd turned into the wrong animal.

One clue to which animal he *had* become this time was that, even though he was now caked in it, Malcolm seemed to really quite like the feel of all this mud. He could feel it sticking to his skin, but instead of thinking *urrrgh* or *I must have a bath* or even, like he would've done when he'd been a cat, *Quick! Lick it off!*, he thought – in more or less the same tone as Homer Simpson might use if he was thinking about doughnuts – *Hmmmm*. Mud…

The other clue was that, bearing down on him as he rolled around in the mud, was an enormous pink two-pin plug socket, with hair coming out of it.

This became a clearer clue when the enormous pink two-pin plug socket with hair coming out of it snorted.

Ah, thought Malcolm. *It's not an enormous pink two-pin plug socket with hair coming out of it. It's a nose. Or, to be more exact, a snout.* The snout moved backwards to reveal that it was attached to the head, and body, of a very large pig indeed, who was looking at him curiously.

"That's odd," said the pig. "Ludwig!"

"Yes, Mabel?"

Malcolm looked round, to see another pig, even more enormous, sitting – well, sprawling – in an even muddier section of what Malcolm now realised was the pigsty.

"Have we had any new kids recently?"

Ludwig thought about this for some time. Then he let out a large grunt. Which Malcolm heard as:

"No. I don't *believe* so…"

"No, I don't think so either. But look."

"Look at what?"

"Ludwig! Come here!"

Ludwig groaned, and heaved himself slowly up

out of his puddle. Large globs of muddy water came off his belly, which seemed to swing in slow motion as he walked across to Malcolm.

Malcolm sat up out of the mud. Well, his bottom half was still very much in the mud. But his face was out of it, at least.

"Hmm…" said Ludwig. "I don't remember this one at all. Especially not the blue eyes. Does he have a name?"

"Excuse me…" said Malcolm. Then he stopped.

"Yes?" said Ludwig.

"Am I a pig?" he said.

"That's a funny question," said Mabel. "None of our children have ever asked that before."

"Yes," said Ludwig. "Although you could say it's a very *good* question. When do any of us truly *become* a pig? Is it when you first roll upside down with your hooves in the air while sinking in the mud? Or is it when you gobble more than seven manky apples in a row?"

"When you do your first really big snort?" suggested Mabel.

"Yes, that is a key moment. Or: is it something more *spiritual* than that? Perhaps it comes with the realisation that it's very unlikely that you will ever fly?"

Mabel sighed, and looked up at Ludwig lovingly. "Oh, Ludwig. You are a very clever pig."

"Some humans, Mabel, have a thing called a Barmitzvah, which marks the date when you become a man. Perhaps we should have something like that. A Pigmitzvah. To celebrate when a piglet becomes a pig."

Malcolm decided the time had come to butt in. "Yes, but they are the humans who don't like pigs."

Ludwig stared at him.

"You say that, but what you mean is they don't *eat* pigs. A good thing, in my book."

Mabel sighed again.

"You're so full of wisdom, Ludwig..." She turned

to Malcolm. "*You* are a lucky piglet. Your father is the cleverest of all pigs, and pigs are the cleverest of all the animals."

"Well," said Malcolm, "if you *are* so full of wisdom, and not just manky apples…"

"Rude," said Ludwig. "We'll have to work on that, Mabel…"

"…then explain why you've got me so wrong. You see: I'm not your child. I'm not a pig. I'm a human. I'm a boy-human. And I *have* a name: Malcolm."

Ludwig and Mabel exchanged glances.

"Well…" said Ludwig, "…it must be awful to feel something so wrong. So first of all, we shall not call you Malcolm. It is a human name."

"Yes, that's because I am human. I just told you."

"I am trying to relieve you of that strange and painful delusion. And also of that name, which is a slightly dated one for a boy at that."

"I beg your pardon?" said Malcolm.

"Well, it is," said Mabel. "It's like Alan. Or Norman. It sounds like you're fifty-four and work as a regional manager for ASDA."

"Please don't mention the human supermarkets," said Ludwig. "We know what products they contain."

"Sorry."

"So," said Ludwig, turning back to Malcolm, "to help you restore pride in your pigginess, and bring you back to loving your piggy-self, we shall call you the most prized pig-name of all…"

"Right," said Malcolm, wearily, "and what is that?"

Ludwig took a deep breath, and said, grandly: "Fatty Bum-Bum!!"

"All hail Fatty Bum-Bum!" said Mabel. "Say it loud and say it proud: Fatty Bum-Bum!"

"Please don't call me that!"

"It's a lovely name!" said Mabel.

"Not if you're a human!"

"Ah, but that is what you need to *stop* thinking

about yourself. Love your pigginess, Fatty Bum-Bum! Love your piggy piggy pigginess, Fatty Bum-Bum!"

As he said this, Ludwig began circling Malcolm, and chanting it. Mabel joined in, circling and chanting. Their hooves splashed mud on Malcolm as they trotted round him, forming a circular pig wall.

"Love your pigginess, Fatty Bum-Bum! Love your piggy piggy pigginess, Fatty Bum-Bum! Love your piggi—"

"Yeah, thing is, pigs…" said a familiar drawling voice, "…he's right. He's *not* a pig."

Malcolm tried to look over Mabel and Ludwig to see who was speaking, but he was too small. So he looked under them, which had its own challenges, given the amount of teats Mabel had, and the amount of mud, straw and bits of manky apple on Ludwig's underside.

But even through all that, he could see – and was mightily pleased to see – Zsa-Zsa the cat, sitting on the wall of the sty. Licking herself, obviously.

CHAPTER TWENTY-SIX

Bring me a manky apple

Next thing Malcolm knew, Trotsky had jumped over the wall of the sty and landed in the mud, looking very pleased with himself.

"Malcolm!" he said, speaking cat, but very much in his excited dog voice. "Malcolm Malcolm Malcolm Malcolm!! Do youzzz remember me? Do youzzz remember me?"

"Yes," said Malcolm.

"What about us?"

"Yes! Us!"

"Us. Us three!"

Malcolm looked up, knowing what he was going to see: the heads of the three Dollys, poking over the sty wall.

"What do you mean, cat?" said Ludwig. "When you say this pig is a boy?"

"Well…" said Zsa-Zsa.

"Hold on," said Malcolm. "How come you can speak to each other? Do you speak pig as well?"

"No," said Mabel. "Ludwig speaks cat. He speaks all the 'malanguages."

"The what?"

"The 'malanguages. Short for animalanguages."

"Yes," said Ludwig, grandly. "I do." He then said, "I do" in cat, tortoise, sheep and dog. All of them sounded to Malcolm just like the words "I do", said over and over again. Except when he said it in dog, which Malcolm didn't understand because he hadn't been one. It sounded a bit like he was saying "sausages", but Malcolm thought it was best not to say that, as he thought it wasn't a word Ludwig would like much.

"Anyway," said Zsa-Zsa, "the point is—"

"And us!"

"Yes, we're here too!"

"Yes! Or at least, on our way!"

Malcolm looked round. It was Benny and Bjornita's voices, but he couldn't see them. He could hardly hear them.

"Don't worry," said Zsa-Zsa, "they're halfway across the field. They'll get here eventually. So. Point is – well, you explain, Malcolm."

So Malcolm explained the whole thing to Ludwig and Mabel: the situation with K-Pax, his transformation into all the animals he'd been so far, the fact that he had been given three days – with two remaining – to find a way of getting back to being human, and the possibly unnecessary information that during his time as a sheep he had been convinced he was about to be made into chops when in fact he was only getting sheared.

"Hmm…" said Ludwig. "I have never seen K-Pax. But I too have heard stories about this goat."

"That he turns people into animals?" said Malcolm.

"No," said Ludwig. "Stranger than that." He

leant in closer to Malcolm, whispering. "That like a human… like, indeed, Gavin the human…"

"Yes?" whispered Malcolm.

"He has a *beard*!"

Malcolm nodded. "Yes. Well. He does. But—"

"Oh my goodness! It is true!"

"No, but—"

"And a moustache?"

"Not really."

"Oh."

"Look, never mind the facial hair. Can you talk to K-Pax? See if you can persuade him to undo the spell? He won't speak to me."

Ludwig looked for a second slightly embarrassed. "No. I'm afraid goat is the one 'malanguage I've never mastered. It's very tricky. Lot of back-of-the-throat hawing."

"Right. So. What should we do?" said Malcolm.

"It's an unusual situation, certainly. It requires all

of my great wisdom."

"Thank heaven then that you are a pig of great wisdom," said Mabel.

Ludwig turned, and began walking up a series of piled-up logs on to the top of the pigs' sleeping area, a small hutch in the middle of the sty. The rest of the animals waited and watched, with bated breath. Ludwig reached the flat surface of the hutch. He stopped. He sat down. He surveyed them all, puffed out his chest, and said:

"Bring me… a manky apple!!"

"Will you…" said Mabel, "…use the manky apple to cure the boy of his pigginess?"

"No!" said Ludwig.

"Will you…" said Bjornita, "…use the manky apple to convince K-Pax to change the spell?"

"No!" said Ludwig.

"Will you…" said Dolly 1.

"Yes, will you…" said Dolly 2.

"I say, will you…" said Dolly 3.

"Look," said Ludwig, "I'm hungry. I can't think straight on an empty stomach. Bring me the stupid apple. And make it manky!!"

Trotsky jumped up, rooted around in the trough, brought out an apple[34] in his mouth, bounded up to the roof of the hutch, and dropped the apple in front of Ludwig. Who proceeded to eat it, slowly, and with a big "I'm thinking" look on his face.

"Excuse me!" said Malcolm, while this was going on. "I don't know what the best thing to do is. But I think if I can just go home… if I can just get to my mum and dad… they'll know what to do."

Over to the west, the sun was beginning to set behind a small wood.

His second day was running out.

At this point, Malcolm felt like he might cry, but

---

[34] It was very manky: bruised on all sides, almost completely brown, with a bite already taken out of it, and covered with mud.

he didn't want to cry in front of all the animals. Luckily, he didn't, because pigs don't have tear ducts. So he just said, his piglet voice breaking a little: "Yes. I'm sure they will."

All the other animals looked on with concern. Apart from Ludwig, who while Malcolm had been talking had just been snuffling loudly around the manky apple. It was now finished, although a bit of manky core was still stuck to his snout.

"Right," said Ludwig, looking up. "To the horses!"

CHAPTER TWENTY-SEVEN

Oh-so-clever pig

"**W**e're still coming!" said Benny.

"We're on our way, don't worry!" said Bjornita.

"Yes, nearly ther— Hang on, where are you lot going?"

"Sausages, sausages, sausages," said Trotsky. But they were already well past the tortoises.

"Oh, for crying out loud," said Bjornita, beginning to turn round. "They're heading for the horses!"

It took a little while for all the animals to get to the horse field. Trotsky was there first, followed by Zsa-Zsa. Then the Dollys arrived, but they didn't stop and carried on running past, quite a long way. Trotsky ran after them, shouting, "Come back, come back!" but – possibly because the sheep didn't speak dog – they just carried on running away. Eventually he had to run past them and herd them back to where they were meant to be.

Luckily, this meant that Ludwig and Mabel and indeed Malcolm had enough time to catch up, arriving just as the sheep came back. Malcolm himself had found it difficult to keep up, as he was only a piglet, with tiny little piglet legs (carrying quite a fat little piglet body).

Ludwig stopped and surveyed the scene. Malcolm tried to see as best he could, above the fence posts. He thought he could make out, through the wire and grass, five horses in there – two brown, two black and one white.

"Right, Fatty Bum-Bum!" said Ludwig. "What we need to do is—"

"Please don't call me Fatty Bum-Bum."

"No, but I have explained to you that I am trying to make you embrace your pigginess."

"And I've explained to you: I'm a boy. Called Malcolm. That's why we're here, by the horses. Isn't it? You've got a plan to get me back to my human parents..."

There was quite a long pause after this, while Ludwig coughed and snuffled and looked around. Eventually, Mabel said:

"I think he's right, Ludwig."

"All right, Mabel. No need to rub it in."

"Ha-ha-ha," said Zsa-Zsa, "the oh-so-clever pig, the cleverest of all the animals, got confused!"

"Shut up, cat! Right. OK. Let's start again. Ahem. So..." Ludwig took a deep breath. Then he let it out again. "Look, can I call you Fatty Bum-Bum anyway? It's such a nice name."

"Malcolm."

Ludwig sighed, with a sense of 'you don't know what you're missing'. "So... Malcolm," he said. "Here's my plan. You go to sleep. You wake up as a horse. Then you run home to your parents."

Trotsky and the Dollys made admiring noises[35] about this plan.

Mabel sighed with love and awe. Even Zsa-Zsa looked impressed. And she – like all cats – never looked impressed.

"Yes. It's a good idea," said Malcolm, choosing not to mention that he'd thought of it ages ago. "OK. I'll give it a try."

And with that, he rolled on to his side, put a hoof under his head, and shut his eyes.

---

[35] A low positive yelp and three small baas.

CHAPTER TWENTY-EIGHT

Whaaaaaaaaarrggggghhh...!!

However, after five minutes, Malcolm could feel he was very much still awake. He opened his eyes.

"What's wrong?" said Ludwig.

"I can't sleep," said Malcolm.

"You can't sleep?" said Mabel.

"No," he said. "I'm normally good at sleeping. And when I was a cat, I was extra-good at it." Zsa-Zsa looked smug about this. "But I think I've been doing too *much* sleeping since I became an animal. I don't feel tired at all."

"Hmm…" said Ludwig. "We'll just have to sing you a lullaby!"

"Really?"

"Yes. It's the one we've sung to all our children. Close your eyes again, please…"

Malcolm did as he was told. And then he heard Ludwig singing, in a low voice, to a lullaby-like tune, these words:

Go to sleep, little piggy
Dream of mud, little piggy
And apples so manky…

Then Mabel joined in, about an octave higher:

Go to sleep, little piggy
Curl up like your tail, little piggy
Be as still as a piggy banky…

Then all the animals joined in. The sheep were actually *harmonising*.

Sleep, sleep, sleep, little piggy
Don't worry about snoring, little piggy
Because the noise you make all the time
Is a bit like snoring, anyway…

Then, just Ludwig again, with a big operatic flourish:

It's snorting!!
Which is like snoring!!
Like snooooorrrrri—

"No, sorry," said Malcolm, opening his eyes, and cutting off Ludwig's final long note. "I don't think that's going to work."

"Oh," said Ludwig. "It always does normally."

Malcolm looked out on to the field. Behind

the horses, he could see that the sun was almost completely down now. Only a few red rays shone through the trees.

"I think… we haven't got time to wait until I'm sleepy. If the three-days thing is right, I've only got two nights left…"

Ludwig took this in. Mabel and Trotsky and Zsa-Zsa and the Dollys all looked stumped. Then Ludwig turned to the field, and shouted:

"Snowflake! Snowflake!"

Seconds later, the ground was shaking – and seconds after that, the white horse that Malcolm had only distantly glimpsed had come over to the fence. From his position, near to the ground, the horse looked like a giant fairy-tale horse, one that might at any moment grow a horn, or wings.

"Neigh!" said Snowflake. Malcolm remembered that he hadn't been a horse, so couldn't speak their language.

"Neigh neigh neigh," said Ludwig. "Whinny whinny

long hard blow out through the nostrils shaking my head at the same time whinny whinny neigh."

"Neigh-whinny!" said Snowflake.

"Blue and yellow?" said Ludwig, in his own language.

"Yeah," said Snowflake. "You've just asked me what colour hat my mum wears on a Tuesday."

"Have I?" said Ludwig. "Hmm. I may need to brush up on my horse."

"It's OK. Luckily, I speak pig."

Ludwig looked a little put out by this, but carried on in his own language all the same.

"Fine. How would you like to be ridden by a pig?" said Ludwig.

"What, you? You'd break my back!"

"That's kind of you to say," said Ludwig, who seemed only too pleased when anyone made reference to his weight. "But no." Malcolm felt Ludwig's snout on his back, a type of pointing. "*This* little fellow. Name of Malcolm."

"Malcolm? Sounds like a middle-aged bank manager with three kids who plays squash at the weekends."

"I know. I offered him Fatty Bum-Bum, but…"

"Ludwig," said Malcolm. "Please. We don't have long."

Ludwig sighed, but nodded. "He needs to get to the city. Quickly," he said.

Snowflake looked down. His long nose and his big brown eyes came very close to Malcolm's face. "Why's that, little chap?"

"That's where my mum and dad are," said Malcolm.

"A city farm?"

"No, they're not pigs. They're humans."

Snowflake shook his head. His mane waved in the air. "Is this something to do with K-Pax?" he said.

"Yes!" said Malcolm.

"OK," said Snowflake. "Hold on!"

Malcolm nodded, although he wasn't sure *what* to hold on to. And also, because he didn't have any fingers, *how*. All this came into his mind with a rush as Snowflake's long muzzle burrowed underneath him, and lifted him high into the air.

"OK," said Snowflake, "now *stop* holding on!"

"I'm not holding on! And I don't know how or what to hold on to anywaaaaaaaaaarrgggggghhh...!!"

He said this as Snowflake threw his (Snowflake's, that is) head high in the air, causing his (Malcolm's, that is) body to slide down his long neck, eventually ending up – with a backwards head-over-heels[36] tumble – sitting, with his tiny legs astride the huge horse's body, in the saddle.[37]

"Right!" said Snowflake. "Now hold on again."

"No, but hold on to what? And with whaaaaaaaa aarrgggggghhh...!!" screamed Malcolm, as Snowflake reared up in the air, bolted to the edge of the field, jumped over the fence, and started off at a canter on the path out of the farm.

---

[36] Yes, I know pigs don't have heels.
[37] Snowflake wasn't wearing a saddle. In the saddle bit, I mean.

CHAPTER TWENTY-NINE

Well...

As dusk fell on Orwell Farm, Mr Barrington was in the living room looking out of the window. *Animals*, he thought: *what an easy life they have. Eat and sleep and sleep and eat.*

OK, sometimes it was eat and sleep and get eaten. But the ones that were kept for milk or wool, or to show to children, like most of the ones on Orwell Farm... Mr Barrington couldn't help envying them a little. Being a human – certainly being a grown-up (a *very* grown-up: Mr Barrington wasn't seeing fifty-nine again), in charge of a large group of Year Six children, was such hard work sometimes.

It had been a long day: the children had been pretty rowdy since the sheep-shearing. Particularly the boys who'd chased the sheep back to their field. They had hardly calmed down since.

Still: they were brushing their teeth now, and getting into their pyjamas. Mr Barrington was looking forward to them all being in bed. Then maybe he could settle down on the sofa with a Sudoku puzzle and a tiny drop of whisky from the flask he had brought with him.

Suddenly, his mobile phone went.

"Hello?"

"Hello, Mr Barrington. It's Malcolm Bailey's father. Stewart."

"Oh yes, hello."

"Is Malcolm there?"

"Er… Malcolm. Yes. I'm sure he is. They're upstairs, I'll just go and—"

"Mr Barrington! Mr Barrington!" He looked up from the phone. Two of the pupils were running into the living room, waving their hands frantically. Mr Barrington squinted at them. They were wearing identical pyjamas. They looked like the same person. But that couldn't be right. He would have to go to his optician again.

"Sorry, I'm on the phone, er…"

"Ellie. It's Ellie."

"And I'm her twin brother, Fred!"

"Oh yes. Yes. Anyway…"

"But… look, Mr Barrington! Out there!"

Mr Barrington looked out of the window again. All he could see was what he'd seen before: the field outside the farmhouse; the gathering dusk; the trees in the distance; and…

"What's that?"

"Yes!"

"That white blur! What is it?"

"It's a horse, Mr Barrington. A white horse! Being ridden by a tiny piglet!"

Mr Barrington frowned and leant closer to the window.

"Are you sure?"

"Yes!"

"So what's that behind it?"

"It's a whole group of animals chasing the horse!" said Fred.

"Which animals?" said Mr Barrington.

"A dog, a cat…"

"Three sheep…"

"Oh, look, two other bigger pigs…"

"And what's that? In the distance…?"

"Is it… two tortoises?"

"Impossible to tell from here."

"Can you see, Mr Barrington?"

"No. No, I can't see. Not in this light, you know. Anyway… Have either of you seen Malcolm?"

Ellie shook her head. "Actually no, I haven't seen him for a little while."

"Last time I saw him was yesterday just before tea, out near the goat pen," said Fred.

Mr Barrington picked up the phone again. "Sorry, Mr Bailey… Hello?"

All he could hear at the other end was:

"BRRRR! HAHAHHA!! HAHAHAHA!! BRRRR!! HAAAHHHAA!"

"Mr Bailey?" said Mr Barrington. "Do you want to speak to Malcolm?"

"No, it's OK… BRRR! HAHAHA!" said Stewart. "You're all clearly having a fabulous time! I don't want to interrupt all your crazy storytelling! Making up all sorts of goings-on at that farm! A piglet riding a horse!"

In the background, Mr Barrington heard

someone say: "LOLT2000!"

"BRR! HAAA! Brilliant!"

"Well…" said Mr Barrington, who frankly remained unsure whether Fred and Ellie had been making it up or not, and therefore could not think of what to say except, "Well…" And then: "Thank you."

Mr Barrington hung up the phone. *I'm getting too old for this*, he thought.

CHAPTER THIRTY

Cute but sad and lost

"How's it going?" shouted Snowflake, above the loud clippety-clop coming from the tarmac.

Malcolm sat up. They'd been going for hours, down country lanes and then bigger roads and now this suburban street, and he was more confident with his riding now. He had found that if he pushed his front hooves along the back of the horse's neck, the little gap in them acted like fingers round Snowflake's luxurious mane. He looked around.

They were riding through streets lit by lamp-posts and the odd light shining from bedroom windows of houses they passed. Behind him, he could see Trotsky, Zsa-Zsa, Mabel, Ludwig and the Dollys doing their best to keep up. It was a warm night, and Malcolm could feel the breeze on his snout and twitching ears.

As they rounded a corner, Malcolm saw a man coming out of a pub. The man's gaze followed Malcolm and Snowflake, and then the gaggle of other animals in their wake. He stood there for a bit, then shook his head, and went back into the pub.

"Great!" shouted Malcolm back.[38]

About an hour later, they were in the city proper. It was night-time now: a pale crescent moon shone above. Snowflake had slowed from a trot to a walk, making it easier for the other animals to follow him.

---

[38] To Snowflake, not the man inside the pub.

And then, suddenly, at a crossroads, he stopped.

"Where should we go?" he said, twisting his neck to look back at Malcolm.

"Sorry?" said Malcolm.

"How do we get to your house?"

Malcolm realised that he didn't know the answer to this. He knew where they lived – Bracket Wood – but he didn't know how to get there from where they were.

"Um… well… where are we now?"

"I don't know," said Snowflake. By this time, Trotsky, Zsa-Zsa, Mabel, Ludwig and the Dollys had caught up. They all stood by the crossroads, looking right and left.

"You don't?" said Malcolm.

"No! I've just been going towards the city. I thought *you* might be able to fill in the details when we got there…"

"Why did you think that?"

"Because, Malcolm…" said Ludwig, butting in,

"Snowflake is an animal. As…" he added, looking at the pig, sheep, dog and cat around him, "…are we all. But you, even though you *look* like a tiny piggy, are apparently a human. So *you* should know stuff like that."

Malcolm looked down from Snowflake's back at the animals looking up at him. He felt terrible at the thought that he'd brought them all here without really knowing what he was doing. He tried – tried hard – to remember something about the geography of the city, but it was difficult, not least because his memory of *being* a human now felt further away than ever.

Then he thought of something.

"What day is it?" he said.

"Huh?" said Ludwig.

"We don't really know stuff like that," said Mabel. "We're animals."

"Yes, I got that," said Malcolm. "You never know

what day it is?"

"Well, to be honest, until you arrived, Malcolm, one day was very much like the next."

"I didn't even know there was such a thing as different days!" said Dolly 1.

"Each day the same!" said Dolly 2. "Grass, grass, grass, sleep, big baa, grass."

"No change from one day to the next!" said Dolly 3.

"It's Sunday," said Zsa-Zsa, somewhat contemptuously. "Early Sunday morning."

All the others looked at her.

"How do you know that?" said Malcolm.

"Because Gavin and Maven always get up later on Sundays, so I get fed later. About ten o'clock. And I can feel my stomach's set for that today. Which is lucky, as otherwise I'd be off back to the farm by now for my brekker."

The other animals looked doubtful. Trotsky

muttered something about, "Allzz ze cat everrr zinks about izzz food."

Malcolm looked over to the side of the road. He could see a newsagent just beginning to open up. The man inside didn't notice them because he was busy piling newspapers up in front of the shop. But Malcolm saw, even with his little piglet eyes from a distance, that the newspapers were thicker than normal. And that brought a memory – a nice memory – back to him: of his parents reading lots of different pages of newspaper on a certain morning, every week…

"Zsa-Zsa's right!" said Malcolm. "It's Sunday. OK, Snowflake, guys – can we just head on into the city? I know where to go!"

"They've stopped," said Benny, breathlessly.

"Yes. They're only about five hundred metres away. Speed up!" said Bjornita.

"I have sped up!"

"Oh. Yes. So have I…"

"Can you speed up a bit more?"

"I'm already going at nearly 10 *metres an hour*. Who do you think I am, Usain Bolt?"

"Oh no! They've started going again."

Half an hour later, the animals (not including the tortoises) were on the outskirts of what looked like a big park. During the journey, Malcolm had turned into a proper rider, tapping Snowflake on his right or left flank whenever he wanted him to turn (right or left, obviously). The other animals had kept on their trail.

Malcolm had been following signs. He'd noticed that his reading wasn't as good as usual – he assumed this was another side effect of being an animal – but luckily the word he'd been looking for on the signs was a small one, and he could still understand it.

"What does that say, Ludwig?" said Dolly 1, as they stood outside the park entrance.

"Yes, what say, Ludwig?"

"Ludwig – that word what?"

"Ahem," said Ludwig, "though I am a very wise pig…"

"The wisest…" said Mabel.

"And the fattest," said Zsa-Zsa.

"Thank you," said Ludwig, "and can speak all the 'malanguages…"

"Apart from horse," said Snowflake.

"Or goat," said Malcolm.

"Yes… anyway, despite that, I haven't quite managed to master the human thing. The words and what they mean."

"Reading," said Malcolm.

"Yes. I rely instead on my native wisdom, unsullied by outside influences, so that my insights have a kind of purity, a native—"

"Zoo," said Malcolm.

"Pardon?" said Ludwig.

"Yes, pardon?" said Mabel.

"Pardon?" said Dolly 2.

"Pardon?"

"Pardon?"

"Oh, for heaven's sake," said Zsa-Zsa, "it sounds like someone's done twenty burps."

"That's what this place is: a zoo."

"What is that?" said Snowflake, sniffing at the ground under the sign.

Malcolm walked down Snowflake's neck, and then jumped off his head. He turned and looked at the animals.

"It's a place with animals. Where my family come every Sunday. Although normally without me. I haven't been since I was six! I can't quite remember why…"

"Right," said Ludwig. "And how do we get in?"

Malcolm looked around. He could see it was getting lighter. He could hear, in the distance, birds singing.

"Morning! It's morning! Morning, morning, morning!"

It sounded like a sweeter version of the cockerel's shouting.

Which made something occur to Malcolm. Maybe K-Pax's spell *required* a cockerel crowing. Maybe the time he had to get back to being human would extend, as long as the actual sound of cock-a-doodle-do didn't enter his ears. *Maybe*, he thought, *if I don't actually* hear—

"WAKE UP! WAKE UP, EVERYBODY! IT'S TIME TO WAKE UP! WAKEY-WAKEY, CHIMPS!! WAKEY-WAKEY, ELEPHANTS!! WAKEY-WAKEY, GIRAFFES!"

"Is that… a cockerel?" said Malcolm, in a deadpan voice.

"It sounds like it," said Ludwig. "Would there be

one in this place?"

"Maybe. Yes. Oh, yes…" said Malcolm, remembering something. "In the petting zoo."

"Sorry?" said Ludwig.

"It's a bit of the zoo where they keep smaller animals for young humans to stroke… I think in there they…"

"WAKE UP, HIPPOS! WAKE UP, REPTILES! WAKE UP, CAMELS!"

"…have chickens and stuff, yes."

It was, clearly, a cockerel. Which meant that this was his last day of trying out being an animal: next time he heard a cockerel crow he wouldn't be trying out being an animal any more. He would *be* one. For good.

He had to think of a way of getting into the zoo. So he could find his parents. Who, he was still assuming, would somehow know what to do.

Then Malcolm had an idea. He looked at all the

animals, and said: "You know that facial expression? The one animals do a lot of the time… that one where you look cute but sad and lost?"

The animals all nodded. And did the expression.

"OK, let's all stand here, face the entrance, and *do* that expression…"

They all did.

"What now?" said Ludwig, with a bit of difficulty, as he didn't want to change his sad, lost expression.

"We wait," said Malcolm.

CHAPTER THIRTY-ONE

A horse, a piglet, two bigger pigs, three sheep, a cat and a dog

Fifty-two-year-old Sanjit Hasan and his young assistant Luke had been opening up the City Zoo for ten years now.

They did other jobs at the zoo – fixing signs and cages, handing out maps, cleaning up[39] – but their first task every day was to open the gates.

Sanjit looked forward to it. He often said to Luke

---

[39] Which, especially in the Elephant House, could take a long time.

that opening the gates was like taking a deep healthy breath of morning air, and today was no exception. It was a lovely morning. The sun was rising above the Aviary and, checking his watch, bang on 9.30am he put the key in the lock. He turned it with a satisfying click, then, as ever, he took the right-hand gate, and Luke took the left-hand one, and together they opened them. As the gates began to move, Sanjit always looked out to check the pavement was clear of litter, or anything else that might disturb prospective customers to the zoo on their way in to see the animals.

Sanjit looked out. The pavement was clear of litter. However, what it wasn't clear of, was animals.

He stopped moving the gate, and blinked a couple of times, wondering if maybe today he hadn't woken up properly, and was still dreaming. But even after he had stopped blinking, they were all still there, just sitting, as if waiting. He opened his mouth to speak, but then Luke said, blankly:

"A horse, a piglet, two bigger pigs, three sheep, a cat and a dog."

"Yes," said Sanjit. "I can see that. Hold the gate a minute."

Luke stopped opening his half of the gate. Sanjit looked at his assistant, who he knew not to be the sharpest claw in the lion cage.

Luke looked back at him, and then at the animals again. "Have they got out?"

"Eh?" said Sanjit.

"From the zoo. Do you think they escaped?"

Sanjit frowned. "Er... do we have a horse, a piglet, two bigger pigs, three sheep, a cat and a dog on show at the zoo? I mean: none of them are, y'know, endangered species."

Luke thought about this for some time. "Yeah, but what about the little zoo? The one for kids?"

"The petting zoo, you mean?"

"Yes. That's right."

Sanjit considered this. He couldn't remember exactly which animals were in the petting zoo. There was a cockerel, he knew that, because its infernal shouting always disturbed his morning tea. But he thought it was possible that the list *also* included horses, pigs, sheep, cats and dogs.

And he didn't want to appear less on the case – as regards the possibility of escaped animals – than Luke. And turning to look at the line of cute faces, he did think that they looked quite sad and lost. So he said:

"OK, let's get them in and check."

"OK," said Luke, and carried on opening his half of the gate. Sanjit did the same. And when the gate was completely open, all the animals trooped inside.

CHAPTER THIRTY-TWO

Memories

As the animals were led by Sanjit and Luke towards the petting zoo, Zsa-Zsa said to Malcolm:

"Right. What should we look out for?"

"What do you mean?"

"Your family, Fatty Bum-Bum. What do they look like?"

"Er…" Malcolm thought. He tried to picture them. But it was hard.

"Come on, Malcolm," said Zsa-Zsa.

"I can't remember…" he said quietly. "The longer I've been an animal, the more my human memories seem to be… going…"

Ludwig stopped and turned. "Try, Malcolm," he said, kindly. "I suspect that of all your memories, this is the one you need to hold on to the most."

As Ludwig said this, Malcolm realised that it was true – if he was ever going to get back to being human, the one memory he mustn't lose was the image, somewhere in his mind, of his family.

He realised something else as well. Which was that Ludwig may not have been able to read or write –

and he may have been slightly pompous and absurd – but it was true: he *was* a very wise pig.

So he shut his eyes and thought, thought hard, about what his family were like. And a faint image came back to him, of Stewart and Jackie and Bert and Libby and Grandpa, of them all coming to the zoo together, as he knew they did every Sunday, and going straight to… going straight to…

"Hey, guys!" he said, opening his eyes. "I've remembered something!"

Unfortunately, however, when he had shut his eyes, Malcolm had also stopped walking.

None of the other animals had.

So now they were nowhere to be seen.

CHAPTER THIRTY-THREE

Mud

"What have you remembered?" said a breathless voice behind Malcolm. He turned round, to see Benny and Bjornita approaching.

"Oh, hi! Where have you been?"

"We've been with you all the time!" said Bjornita.

"Well, not *with* you," said Benny. "*Behind* you. Quite a long way behind you."

"As far as I'm concerned," said Bjornita, haughtily, "we've always been operating as part of the group."

"Anyway," said Benny, "*What* have you remembered?"

"Where my family always head to first when they go to the zoo!" said Malcolm, turning round and trotting off as fast as his little legs would carry him, leaving the tortoises far behind again.

"Oh, for heaven's sake," said Bjornita. "I'm off to the reptile house. To see my giant great-aunt."

It wasn't that difficult to find what Malcolm was looking for. He again had to follow signs, but this time the signs had pictures on them to help. The Elephant House arrow had a cartoon elephant on the end of it, the Lion and Tiger Area arrow was decorated with, well, lions and tigers, and the one Malcolm was looking for had, on the end of its arrow, a dancing, crazy, smiling monkey.

He followed the way set out by three of those arrows and ended up in front of the Monkey

House. The cage he was looking at was huge and contained nearly twenty chimpanzees, rolling around and scratching each other and staring into space. It made Malcolm uncertain, watching them. Something about the monkeys[40] was making him feel uncomfortable. But he couldn't quite place it.

Never mind, thought Malcolm. *What about my family?*

He looked away from the cage. It was still early but there were already people in the zoo. A few of them had noticed him as he'd been walking around – he'd heard one grown-up say, "I guess it must be some kind of new initiative, letting some of the animals just roam about" – but so far he hadn't seen anyone he recognised.

Malcolm went to sit on a grassy area just behind the concrete path in front of the chimpanzee enclosure. He had a good view of the chimps from

---

[40] Chimps aren't monkeys. They are apes. However, this distinction had always escaped Malcolm's family. Possibly because of the Monkey Moment.

here and could see any families approaching them.

He settled down on a small muddy patch. *Hmm,* he thought, *mud. How nice.*

And even though he was meant to be keeping a sharp eye out for his family, he soon found himself rolling upside down in the mud, rubbing his head and ears into it, and closing his eyes. It had after all been a long night, travelling all the way there on the back of a big white horse. He'd had no sleep. So it was nice, just for a moment, to let himself sink into this little bit of mud. It was amazing, actually, just how comfy mud was. It was like halfway between a bath and a very soft bed. If you didn't worry about it being dirty – and strangely, Malcolm, as a pig, really didn't – it was just very, very relaxing.

So relaxing, in fact, that Malcolm soon found himself drifting off to sleep, thinking, as he did so, that maybe Fatty Bum-Bum *was* a really nice name after all.

CHAPTER THIRTY-FOUR

Lord King Louie's precious pile of poop

When Malcolm woke up about an hour later, his first thought was: *Oh, I've changed back to being a human. Maybe my mum and dad came down when I was asleep and sorted everything out.*

The reason he thought this was because the first thing he saw when he opened his eyes was his right hand, lying in front of his face – a hand with four fingers and a thumb, lines across the palm, and nails on the fingers. It was a tiny bit... grey, but Malcolm assumed this was because it had got dirty pressed against the mud.

He glanced around, wondering where – if they had sorted everything out – his mum and dad were. He noticed that he still had a good view of the chimps. In fact, if anything, he had a *better* view of the chimps. One particular chimp was right in front of him, his hairy brow furrowed, dangling his hand in front of Malcolm's face.

"What are you doing?" said Malcolm.

"Hold on," said the chimp, "hold still… OK!" The chimp reached out and pinched his fingers on to Malcolm's forehead.

"Got it!" he said.

"Got what?"

"A flea," he said, holding up to the light a tiny insect.

"Yum," he added. And ate it.

At which point Malcolm realised that he wasn't

actually a human again after all. He knew what he was. He stood up and looked around, at the other chimps with him in the enclosure.

"Still," he said out loud, "at least – compared to a pig – in DNA terms, I'm getting closer."

"Funny you should mention that," said the flea-eating chimp, pointing to beyond the cage bars. "There was a little pig out there a while back. Sleeping."

"Was there…" said Malcolm, sitting up, and looking at his own black furry arms, and black and grey furry tummy, and (once again) incredibly human hands.

"Yes. Just behind that bit where all the humans stand, and stare, and point at us, and laugh."

Malcolm looked out. He could see two families standing there, neither of them his own. They were indeed staring, and pointing, and laughing.

It made him think, a little, about how it must be for the animals in here: about how they must feel, being on show all the time; like they were in… well… a zoo.

"What's your name?" said the chimp.

"Malcolm," he said.

The chimp jumped up and down, and chattered his teeth, and made screeching noises.

"Are you laughing at my name?" said Malcolm.

"No, I was just letting off a bit of steam. You know, like you do."

"Oh. What's your name?"

"Tarzan," said Tarzan.

Malcolm jumped up and down, chattered his teeth and made screeching noises.

"You see, it feels great, doesn't it?" said Tarzan.

"No, I was laughing at your name," said Malcolm.

"Oh," said Tarzan, looking a bit cross.

"Sorry, not because it's a silly name. Just because in the human world, Tarzan is the name of a man who's brought up by monkeys."

"We're not monkeys," said Tarzan. "Chimps are apes."

"Oh," said Malcolm.

"How come you don't know that? And how come you know that weird thing about my name?"

"Because I'm a human," said Malcolm. "I'm a boy."

Tarzan jumped up and down, chattered his teeth, and made screeching noises.

"That was you laughing that time, wasn't it?" said Malcolm, after he'd finished.

"Yep," said Tarzan.

After this, another chimp came over, turned round, bent over, and said, "Here's my bum," which Tarzan seemed to take quite badly, and they ended up having a big roly-poly fight. Malcolm decided that while he was waiting for his family to show up, he might as well see what it was like being a chimp.

So he scurried, half bent over, up a wooden ladder on to a high platform standing in the

right-hand corner of the cage. He held up one of his long arms, got hold of one vine hanging from the ceiling, and swung halfway across the cage; then leapt from there to another one, and swung the rest of the way across.

He jumped from that one on to another high platform in the left-hand corner, and climbed halfway down to an enormous tyre swing. He sat in the tyre swing, and let Tarzan, whose fight had stopped almost as suddenly as it had begun,[41] push him. He swung high, sticking his legs out (noticing that his feet too, though hairy, were very human). After about twenty swings, he let himself fall off, on to a rope net below. The rope net turned out to be quite tightly strung, and landing on it created a big bounce, like a trampoline, throwing Malcolm halfway back across the enclosure.

---

[41] Although the other chimp was still bending over and showing Tarzan his bum. It just didn't seem to bother Tarzan any more.

Being a chimp, thought Malcolm, while he was in the air, *is brilliant.*

It's like being in the best playground ever, except that you're more able than usual to swing and climb and jump. I love it, he thought. Well, actually, he thought *I love—*

He never got as far as the *it*, because that was when he landed right on the back of the head of the biggest chimp in the cage.

"Owwwww!" said the biggest chimp in the cage.

"Sorry!" said Malcolm, rolling away.

"Sorry won't stop my head hurting!" the big chimp shouted, in a deep booming voice.

"Sorry!" said Malcolm again.

"I said—"

"Yes, but I don't know what else to say!"

"Also you have disturbed Lord King Louie's precious pile of poop!" said another smaller chimp to the side of the scarily big one.

"I beg your pardon?"

"Lord King Louie's precious pile of poop!!" said a second chimp.

"Oh my goodness! The Holy Plop-Plop!" said a third one.

Malcolm looked down: by his feet, there was a small pyramid of what looked like chimp poo, which did indeed look a little disturbed. It looked a little like, in fact, one of the real pyramids.[42]

When he looked up, the three chimps all jumped up and down, chattering their teeth and screeching. But they clearly weren't laughing. They were cross with Malcolm; and approaching Malcolm. Crossly.

Uh-oh, he thought.

---

[42] In that it had a big dent in it. Not in that the pyramids are made out of poo.

CHAPTER THIRTY-FIVE

Dominant male

"**S**ee-No! Speak-No! Hear-No! It's fine!" said Louie. "I'm fine."

The three chimps stopped jumping, chattering and screeching immediately. Instead, they lowered their heads, bowed towards Louie, and backed off, saying:

"Thank heavens for that, Your Eminence…"

"Truly thankful, Your Chimpi-nence…"

"Could not be more relieved, Your Hairy-ness…"

"Now…" said Louie, turning to Malcolm, his voice more booming and low than ever, "who *are* you? And *why* have you disturbed my mid-morning sleep?"

"Well, Louie…" said Malcolm.

"*Lord King* Louie!" interjected See-No.

"Or Your Chimpi-nence!" said Speak-No.

"And if you *continue* to speak to the Lord King, it's *ch'amp* as in Champion Chimp, not Ch'ump as in –" at this point Hear-No looked a bit uncertain – "chump."

"Er… right. Well, Lord King Louie, sir…"

"You don't have to say sir," said Louie, magnanimously.[43]

"Right. Well. Thing is, I'm a…" Suddenly, Malcolm felt very tired of having to explain about how he was really a boy again. Also, for some reason he couldn't quite explain, he was not particularly keen on Louie. So instead he said…

---

[43] This is a word that means "generously but also grandly, like a king granting a favour to a peasant". I could have said that, but it would have taken a bit long. Then again, if you've read this footnote, it's taken even longer.

"Actually, *why* do I have to call you Lord King Louie? And why is everyone bowing and scraping to you?"

Louie frowned – chimps can *really* do this – and very large lines appeared across his forehead. His nostrils flared, becoming even wider holes than they already were. Speak-No, Hear-No and See-No looked incredibly shocked – in fact Speak-No put both his hands over his mouth, Hear-No put his over his ears, and See-No put his over his eyes.

"Because I..." said Louie, even more loudly and boomingly, "...am the Dominant Male in this community!"

"The Dominant Male!" echoed Speak-No, Hear-No and See-No together (still holding their hands over their mouth, ears and eyes – so it was quite hard to hear Speak-No, and quite surprising that Hear-No heard it in the first place).

Then they actually sang it, like an *amen* in church:

"*The dooh-minn-annt…*

Ma-yalll!"

"Would you like to dispute my dominance, *Malcolm?*" said Louie, rising up to his full height. "*Would you like to challenge it?*"

Louie then did something, which, if Malcolm hadn't been so frightened, he might have found funny, as it was so… *monkey-ish*.

He – Louie[44] – raised both his long, furry arms above his head, and brought his fists down on his chest, beating it repeatedly, and screaming while he did it, like a… well, like a big monkey. Like King Kong.

Suddenly, *all* the chimps in the enclosure were surrounding Louie and Malcolm, going:

"Fight! Fight! Fight! Fight!"[45]

Louie was still beating his chest. Malcolm – although he didn't really want to fight – thought:

---

[44] Or His Chimpiness the Lord King Louie, if any of you reading are chimps.

[45] Apart from one chimp, a female one, called Tracey, who was going: "Don't do it, Louie! He's not worth it!"

oh well, when in Rome. Or rather: *when in the Monkey Drome*.

So he raised himself up to *his* full height, and started beating *his* chest and screaming, too.

It kind of felt good. It kind of felt *right*. It kind of made Malcolm feel he was up for the fight. *Hey*, he thought, *maybe if I win this fight, I'll be the Dominant Male, and all the others will have to call* me, *Your Chimpiness! That'll be great.*

They approached each other, fists-a-beating, with all the other chimps still going: "Fight! Fight! Fight!"

Louie raised one of his fists above his head. Malcolm – suddenly realising that taking on the much bigger Louie may have been a mistake – cowered. But then, just before Louie brought that fist down on Malcolm, Hear-No cried out: "Your Smelliness!"

"What is it!?" said Louie.

"A human boy! Approaching the cage!"

Louie and all the other chimps stopped what they were doing immediately, turning to look. Louie nodded, and took a deep breath.

"We will deal with *this*…" he said, looking heavily at Malcolm, "…later. Meanwhile: prepare yourselves… for the ritual!!!"

The chimps all scurried away, as if taking positions.

Malcolm, confused, turned to look at the bars of the cage.

There, standing on the other side of them, smiling, pointing and clapping, was his little brother, Bert.

CHAPTER THIRTY-SIX

Oh dear

"I love the zoo so much!" said Jackie, as they approached the Monkey House.

"Yes!" said Stewart. "So do I!"

"Yeah. The zoo is, like, ZOO," said Libby.

"What does that one mean?" said Grandpa.

"Zillion OMGs. Obvs…"

Grandpa nodded. "I sometimes wonder if you are just making these up on the spot."

"Look at Bert!" said Jackie. "He's run up ahead!"

"He's loving the chimps!" said Stewart.

"Can I eat them?" shouted Bert. "Can I eat them?"

"Should we let him go so close to the bars?" said Jackie. "You know we haven't let any of the children do that since..." she faltered a little, lowering her voice: "...the Monkey... Moment."

"Oh, I think it'll be fine. Just keep an eye out," said Stewart. "Talking of Malcolm," he continued, taking Jackie's hand as they walked, "I feel sure from the phone calls that he's having *such* a good time on the farm that when he comes back we can bring him here again! I think he'll be over the Monkey Moment, and find his love for animals once more!"

"Ah…" said Jackie, sadly. "I hope you're right." By this point, they were standing in front of the Chimp Enclosure. Jackie turned towards it and said: "I just wish he was here now."

Malcolm looked at Bert, and behind him, his mum, dad, grandpa and sister. He ran over to the bars of the cage.

"Mum! Dad! Bert! Grandpa! Libby!" he shouted, pointing to himself. "It's me! Malcolm!"

"Oh look, Bert! Look at that one!" said Grandpa. "He's jumping up and down and pointing at himself! What do you think he's saying with all that screaming?"

"I think he's saying… eat me! You can eat me, if you want!"

"No, I don't think so, Bert…"

"Is he saying this?" said Bert. He'd managed to pick Stewart's pocket. In his hand, he held up Stewart's phone, with the AnimalSFX app onscreen. He pressed the chimp icon. It made a chattering noise.

The family all laughed.

"Oh, for heaven's sake!" shouted Malcolm. "No. That icon is not even speaking proper monkey. Bert! Libby! It's me, Malcolm!"

"Wow," said Libby, sounding ever-so-slightly un-bored for a moment, "that monkey is, like, so GOI!"

"GOI?" said Grandpa.

"Going on Instagram!" said Libby, turning round to face away from the cage – pouting, brushing her hair and producing her phone at the same time in one expert move.

"No!" said Malcolm. "You don't understand!"

Click! went Libby's phone. She turned round again, clicking on it.

"Selfie... with monkey... LOLT3000... smiley face smiley face laughing face crying face smiley laughing crying monkey face."

"I don't want to be on Instagram!!" shouted Malcolm. "And: I'm not a monkey!"

"That's right!" shouted Tarzan, from somewhere behind him. "Chimps aren't monkeys! You tell 'em."

"Yes! That's right! But I didn't mean that! I meant... Mum! Dad! I'm Malcolm!"

"Ha-ha! What a funny monkey!" said his mum and dad.

"Chimp!" corrected Malcolm. "And... boy!"

"Look at his silly jumping up and down and pointing at himself! So funny!"

Malcolm looked at them. He stopped jumping up and down and pointing at himself. He took a deep breath, and let out a deep sigh. He felt very sad: he had been so sure that when he found his family they would be able, somehow, to see it was him – that whatever animal he happened to be at the time, they would see through the outer skin, and realise: "Oh my

God: that's *Malcolm*." Instead, they were laughing and pointing and saying what a funny monkey he was.

He turned round, away from his family.

I suppose, he thought, *I should just rejoin the other chimps. And get used to being one of them for the rest of my* life.

When he turned round, however, he didn't quite have time to just indulge himself in self-pity about this. Because he noticed something about all the chimps. Which was that they had all raised their arms. And they were all holding something.

A trickle formed in Malcolm's memory. A trickle which became a flood when he looked over at Lord King Louie, and remembered why he might not have felt very happy to have made his acquaintance.

Because Lord King Louie was scooping his hand into the pile of Holy Plop-Plop at his feet.

And then raising that hand above his head.

"Remember," shouted Hear-No to all the other

chimps, "the first throw always goes to the Lord King Louie!!"

There were some grumbling noises at this point.

"Stop grumbling!" shouted See-No. "That's how it always goes!"

In that second, it all came back to Malcolm: all the terror and humiliation of the Monkey Moment.

And what made it worse was, as he looked at the angle of Louie's arm, he realised that this time, the chimp was not aiming at him, but at Bert.

"Bert!" shouted Malcolm. "Run! Take cover!"

"Oh good," said Stewart. "That one's perked up again. I thought he'd gone a bit quiet!"

"Can I eat him?" said Bert, opening his mouth.

Opening: his *mouth*.

Oh dear.

CHAPTER THIRTY-SEVEN

Splat

"Right!" said Louie. "Here! We! Go!"

A round ball of Dominant Male poo left his hand, travelling very quickly in the direction of Bert. Realising it was too late to do anything else – and that Bert and the rest of his family were, frankly, too stupid (despite their previous experience) to understand what was happening – Malcolm came to a swift and unhappy conclusion.

Then he jumped in front of Bert, making himself

a human shield.

Sorry, a monkey shield.

Sorry, an *ape* shield.

Splat! went the ball of poo. All over Malcolm's face.

A huge gasp went up from the chimps.

"What! Are! You! Doing?" shouted Louie, furiously.

"Protecting my little brother!" shouted Malcolm back, although he didn't shout it *that* loud, as, just at the minute, he didn't want to open his mouth too wide.

"What is he talking about?" said Louie.

"We've no idea, Your PG-Tips-ness," said Speak-No.

"Never mind. *On with the ritual!*" shouted Louie, picking up more poo from the pile. And throwing it at Bert. Except Malcolm was still standing in front of him.

Splat again!

"I'm warning you, Malcolm…" shouted Louie.

"No!" shouted Malcolm.

"Have you seen what all the other chimps are holding?"

"I haven't seen, no," said Malcolm. "As I'm shutting my eyes very tightly. But I can guess!"

"You have one last chance. Step aside!"

As if in answer, Malcolm put his hands behind him and laced his long arms between the bars, to make it clear he wasn't going anywhere.

"Fine!"

Louie nodded to Hear-No, Speak-No and See-No. Who all turned to the massed ranks of the chimps, and screamed, in unison: "Launch… poos!!"

Every chimp in there raised their arms and starting chucking stinky missiles at Bert. The poos flew in not-very-beautiful arcs towards where he was standing.

Malcolm heard his mum say: "Oh my goodness! Not again! Bert! Come away!"

"Yes! Bert!" said his father. "Step away from the cage!"

"GOOTW, Bert!" said Libby, sounding a little un-bored at this moment. "Like: GOOTW!"[46]

But Bert didn't. Because none of the poo had actually hit him yet, he just found it really funny. Malcolm could hear him laughing. And, on the edges of his vision, he could also see him, ducking round to try to get a better view of the funny monkeys trying – as far as Bert was concerned – to throw poo at the one monkey standing in front of him.

So that meant that Malcolm became: a goalie.[47]

He had to dive in front of/block with his body/get his head in the way of about thirty balls of poo.

Bert moves to the right – Malcolm dives to the right: *splat* on his arm!

Bert moves to the left – Malcolm dives to the left: *splat* on his shoulder!

---

[46] Get Out Of The Way

[47] A pooalie?

Bert tries to jump higher than Malcolm (who as a chimp is not taller than him) to see better – Malcolm leaps up and catches another one – *splat*! – full in the face.

Bert crouches down to see through Malcolm's legs – Malcolm kneels down and takes one for the team – well, for Bert, anyway – right in his softest chimp bits.

Splat.

By the end of it, Malcolm was completely covered. It was *much, much* worse than the original Monkey Moment, when at least he'd had the bars of the cage in the way.

But still: Bert was poo-free. And now, surely, his family would realise who this chimp really was, who had saved their youngest son from having his own Monkey Moment.

Malcolm turned round to face them, opening his eyes and his arms wide. He knew he was encrusted in smelliness from head to foot, and that he therefore might not present the loveliest image to his family, but he was convinced that his enormous act of self-sacrifice would mean that they would see through the poo (and the chimp body) and recognise him.

What he saw, instead, were the backs of his family, as they walked away.

"Goodness me," Stewart was saying. "That was a bit weird."

"Yeah," Libby replied, "GROSS."

"Does that mean Get Rid Of Smelly—?" said Grandpa.

"No," interrupted Libby, "it just means gross. Which that was."

"So do the chimps do that to *every* little boy that comes right up to the cage?" Jackie said.

"Maybe," replied Stewart. "Thank goodness for the blocking chimp, though..."

"Yes. I wonder why he was doing that?"

"Oh, just for a bit of chimpy fun, I imagine. They probably love getting covered in poo."

"Can I eat him?"

"Certainly not at the moment, Bert, no."

Malcolm watched them go. He felt very, very sad, and would have started crying, even, had he not been hit on the back of the head at that point by one last poo missile, from one last chimp – which, having had quite a lot of time to harden, knocked him out.

CHAPTER THIRTY-EIGHT

A day over 148

When Malcolm woke up, the first things he saw, looking up at him from the grass opposite the Chimp Enclosure, were Benny and Bjornita.

"Oh no," he thought, "not a *tortoise* again. Please."

"Well, thank you very much, I'm sure!" said Bjornita.

"Did I say that out loud?" groaned Malcolm.

"You did," said Benny. "Interestingly, you said it in tortoise. Otherwise we wouldn't have understood you."

"Yeah, well that's because I *am* a tortoise again…" said Malcolm, reaching out a leg to try to rub his aching head. "Aren't I?"

He said 'aren't I', partly because he realised that what Benny said didn't quite make sense – if he was a tortoise, then why was it interesting that he was speaking tortoise? – and partly because the leg he was reaching out to rub his head with appeared to be… covered in feathers.

"No," said Benny, "you're a pigeon."

"And frankly, your tortoise accent is *terrible*," said Bjornita.

Malcolm stood up – or rather perched up. He looked around. He looked around some more, at a slightly different angle. He looked around the other way.[48] He looked at the sky. The sun was either going up or going down. There was no way to tell.

---

[48] You know. Like pigeons do.

"What happened to my family" he said, in his pigeon[49] tortoise.

"What family?" said Benny.

"Humans. A mum and dad, a teenage girl, a grandpa and a little boy…"

"Would the teenage girl be taking selfies with every animal?" said Bjornita.

"Yes!"

"And would the little boy be asking if he could eat every animal?" said Benny.

"Yes!"

"We just passed them on the way out…"

"Right! Thanks!" said Malcolm, hopping through the bars and joining them on the grass. He spread his wings. It felt good: he could feel the wind underneath them, ready to lift him… and then:

"Wait a minute," he said. "What am I doing?"

---

[49] You could, if you were very clever, spell this PIDGIN.

"Going after your family?" said Benny.

"No, but…" He put his wings down. "They were just here. While I was a chimp. And they didn't recognise me. How will they recognise me as a *pigeon?*"

"That's true," said Benny. "After all, pigeons do look much less like humans than chimps…"

"Oh, that's very helpful," said Bjornita.

"Sorry, but they do."

"And what time is it?" said Malcolm, looking up into the sky.

"We don't have much of a sense of time," said Benny. "It passes a bit slower for us than most…"

"Oh, forget it," said Malcolm. He looked at the sun. It was about halfway between directly up and the horizon. It couldn't be mid-morning, so it must be… mid-afternoon.

Oh no.

"OK," said Malcolm, sounding calmer than he felt. "So in a few hours it'll be dark, and by tomorrow morning it will have been three days since K-Pax transformed me into an animal."

"A tortoise!" said Benny, in an upbeat way, but then realised, looking at Malcolm's sad face, that it probably wasn't the moment for upbeatness.

"Yes," said Malcolm, quietly. "So I may as well sit it out here and just accept that I'm *never* going to get back to being a boy..."

He folded his wings round himself, covering his eyes, and sank down on to the grass. Benny and Bjornita exchanged glances.

Eventually, Bjornita said:

"Malcolm. Listen. I remember when I was a tiny tortoise, and first saw my reflection in a pool of water. I thought: *Urrgh. I'm so ugly.*"

"Bjornita!"

"Shh, Benny, let me carry on. I did. I know it's

hard to believe. Anyway: my first owner then was a little girl called Victoria who used to live on the farm. And Victoria saw me looking into the pool and I don't know if – somehow – she knew I was sad, but just at that moment she came over, lifted me up, kissed me on the head and told me she loved me!"

Malcolm didn't respond. His wings remained wrapped round himself. But the tip of his tiny head was visible, and he was listening. Bjornita continued:

"So the point is, Malcolm – I may not have learned that much in my 149 years on this earth – yes, that's right, Benny, I said it, 149 – but one thing I *have* learned is: it may take a little time, but the ones who love you will *always* be able to see through the outer shell."

There was a short pause.

Malcolm stirred, a little.

Bjornita looked worried.

Then Benny said, sounding panicked:

"Sorry, do you mean shell as in… shell? Like my shell? They can see through it? To my naked body?"

"No," sighed Bjornita. "I mean…"

"I know what you mean," said Malcolm, suddenly looking up. "Thank you, Bjornita. And by the way…" he said, spreading his wings, "you're beautiful: you don't look a day over 148."

And with that, he flew up into the sky.

CHAPTER THIRTY-NINE

EIWKLTSH

One of the really good things about being an animal, Malcolm had discovered, was that there was nothing to learn. All the stuff humans did – drive, cook, read and write, use computers – you had to spend hours and hours studying how to do. But jumping off the farm roof when he had been a cat, or leaping from vine to vine when he had been a chimp – the ability was just *there*. It was part and parcel of animal life.

It was the same, now that he was a bird, with flying.

He just opened his wings and took off. It was amazing. He knew instinctively how to float, how to hover, how to swerve into and out of the wind, how to dive and how to soar. It was a sunny day but with some fluffy clouds, and Malcolm actually flew into one of them! It was like suddenly being in a mist, and then out again, into bright day.

Below him, the zoo looked tiny, like something on Google Earth. Malcolm knew he should be looking for his family, but a part of him couldn't resist just having fun. So he swooped low over the Land of the Lions, seeing them lying asleep on the rocks, and then lower still over Penguin Beach (trying hard not to shout, "Ha-ha, I can fly and you can't!"[50]), and briefly landed on the head of a pygmy hippo, before passing over the petting zoo

---

[50] Although I don't know if penguins understand pigeon. There might be one language for all birds, flying or not. Don't push me on this, I'm not an expert.

and shouting, "I'm going to find my family!" at Zsa-Zsa, Trotsky, Ludwig, Mabel, Snowflake and the three Dollys, who seemed to have all been placed in a holding pen while the zoo worked out what to do with them.

"Hooray!" they all shouted back, apart from Zsa-Zsa, who looked a bit not-bothered – although she looked like that most of the time – and Mabel, who said, "Hang on, is that Malcolm? Is he a pigeon now, then?"

But Malcolm didn't hang around to hear all that. He was off again, rising high over the trees, towards the road that circled the zoo. Most birds at this point during the day – perhaps every single other bird in the world – would be looking for bugs in the air, or worms wriggling on the ground, or possibly a lovely branch on which to begin building a nest.

Malcolm, however, was looking for… a twelve-year-old blue Vauxhall Zafira.

Seeing his family seemed, at least for the moment, to have brought his memory back: his human memory. At least for now, he knew which car his family would be travelling home in. His beady, precise eyes scanned the road from above.

No, he thought, *that one is far too new... that one is working too well... that one hasn't got enough space at the back to carry four or five pet cages when we go on holiday...*

Ah! There it was. Chuntering down the road a bit stop-start because the exhaust was dodgy.

Malcolm flew behind the car, easily following it: his mum was driving, and she never went over thirty miles per hour. In fact, he didn't just follow it: he flew round the car, circling it, dipping down now and then to say "Hello!" to Libby or Bert or Grandpa in the back, but they didn't seem to notice.[51]

---

[51] Although once, obviously, Bert asked if he could eat him.

As the car wound through the streets, Malcolm also found himself shouting, often, to other pigeons, standing around in the road:

"Oy! Get out of the way! Quickly, fly away, fly away!"

"Don't be stupid!" they would shout back. "You must have done this! We all do it! It's like a game of chicken. Last one out of the road's a aaaaargggggghhh—" they would say, hopping or flying out of the Zafira's way at the last minute.

Finally, the car got to number 43 Kendal Road.[52]

It parked up outside.

Malcolm landed on the wall by their front gate, and watched his family get out of the car.

"Mum! Dad! Libby! Grandpa! Bert! It's me!" he said. "Malcolm!"

"Hello!" said Jackie.

---

[52] Told you so. You wouldn't know where we were otherwise, would you?

Malcolm couldn't believe it. He let out a huge: "Oh! Mum! You've recognised me! Oh! I knew you would!"

"What a sweet pigeon, Stewart. Have you seen it? It's singing to us!"

Malcolm let out a small: "Oh no."

"Oh, that is sweet, Jackie," said Stewart. "By the way, who's going to pick up Malcolm later?"

"Oh yes! The school bus is coming back tonight, isn't it? I'll go."

"No, I'm here!" said Malcolm. "Here!"

"I really miss him," continued Jackie. "Can't wait until he's home."

"Yes, me too," said Stewart.

"And me," said Grandpa.

"EIWKLTSH!"[53] said Libby.

"I *don't* want to eat him!" said Bert.

---

[53] Even I Would Kinda Like To See Him. No one really realised she'd said this though, as it sounded like a sneeze.

"Well, Bert!" said Stewart, turning the key. "That's very nice of you…"

They all went into the house. Malcolm watched, with mixed feelings. It was *so* frustrating that they couldn't understand him. But at the same time, it was nice to hear them talk about him like this, without knowing he was there. He thought to himself:

Oh. My family really love me. That's amazing. Even though they're all such big animal fans, and I'm not.

But then that thought led on to another one, which was:

But I don't know that I'm NOT an animal fan any more. I've really liked some of being an animal. And I've really, really liked some of the animals I've met. Not so much the chimps. But the pigs and the sheep and the horse and the tortoises and the dog and the… oh no.

He thought *oh no*, because creeping towards him, along the wall, and licking its lips, was a cat.

But not Zsa-Zsa.

No.

Ticky: out of Ticky and Tacky.

Or was it Tacky?

CHAPTER FORTY

Is this how it ends?

"Listen..." Malcolm started to say, but it was too late. There was no chance to demonstrate his newfound ability to speak cat – pigeon cat, of course, but still cat – because Ticky (or Tacky) was just too quick for him.

He (or she) leapt through the air, and grabbed Malcolm, pulling him off the wall and into the front garden. Her (or his) claws dug into him.

The pain was excruciating.

"Ow! Ow!" Malcolm cried. And then he couldn't speak at all, because Ticky or Tacky had bitten into his neck. Malcolm could feel the fangs going in – not deep enough to kill, because Ticky/Tacky, like all cats, was clearly thinking he/she fancied playing with this bird for a bit longer first – but deep enough to cause even more pain.

He flapped his wings, but it made no difference – one of them already felt useless and broken.

Is this how it ends? thought Malcolm. *Killed by my own cat. And I still don't even know which one.*

CHAPTER FORTY-ONE

This army

And then, just as he felt his body go completely limp and his mind start to turn black, Malcolm heard a voice:

"Step *away* from the pigeon…"

"Eh?" said Ticky. Or Tacky.

"You heard me: step away from the pigeon…"

Malcolm felt the teeth slowly being removed from his aching neck. His head flopped to the other side. His vision was cloudy but he could see, through the mist, standing in front of the gate to 43 Kendal Road,[54] her fur up and her tail raised and her teeth bared: Zsa-Zsa.

"And if I don't…" hissed Tacky or Ticky, "who's gonna make me?"

"Me," said Zsa-Zsa.

"Oh yeah? You and whose army?" As Tacky or Ticky said this, another cat – a brown one; the first one was white – came round the corner of the house and joined Ticky or Tacky. This must be Tacky. *Or Ticky*, thought Malcolm, groaning inside.

Zsa-Zsa blinked, a long, slow blink. And then behind her appeared: Snowflake, Ludwig, Mabel, the three Dollys, Trotsky and even Benny and Bjornita.[55]

"Me…" she said, "and *this* army."

---

[54] Still useful to know this.

[55] Benny and Bjornita had been carried there on Snowflake's back. How did they get up there? Do you know, I'm not entirely sure.

CHAPTER FORTY-TWO

Ticky

"OK… OK…" said the Kendal Road cats, backing away together. Malcolm felt, through the pain, a huge wave of relief.

"But why?" one of them said. "Why are you – a *cat* – trying to save… a *bird*?"

"Well," said Zsa-Zsa, "partly because we've come all this way…"

"And ve had to break out of ze zzzoo to get here…" said Trotsky.

"And use our sense of smell…" said Ludwig.

"Well, yours *is* terribly good."

"Thank you, Mabel… to track where the pigeon went…"

"Yes. But mainly because: he's Malcolm."

The Kendal Road cats stared at Zsa-Zsa. Then at each other. Then back at Zsa-Zsa.

"What do you mean?"

"Yeah, what do you mean?"

"It's a very long story," said Zsa-Zsa. "Which, frankly, I can't be bothered to explain to you now. But this *is* your owner – or one of them, anyway – the boy. Malcolm. Just… in pigeon form."

"I don't believe you," snarled the white cat.

"Neither do I," super-snarled the brown one.

"Well, I don't think that really matters," said Zsa-Zsa, coming further towards them, with the other animals behind. "Because we're taking him now."

"Well…" said the super-snarling one, "I don't

know why you're helping him, even if he *is* Malcolm."

"Huh?" said Zsa-Zsa.

"*Malcolm…*" the brown cat continued, his/her eyes narrowing, "doesn't even like animals. He doesn't like you. He doesn't like ANY OF YOU!"

Malcolm, his head still floppy, tried to speak, tried to explain.

That's not true any more, he wanted to say. But it wouldn't come out.

The Orwell Farm animals looked deeply shocked and upset. Zsa-Zsa frowned. Trotsky put his head down. The three Dollys did some very quiet baa-ing. Eventually, Ludwig came forward – it was a bit of a squeeze for him through the front gate – bent his enormous head down towards the pigeon, and said, quietly:

"Malcolm… is that true? That you don't like animals?"

With all his remaining strength, Malcolm

whispered: "No…"

The farm animals looked relieved. But then the white cat raised its head and said:

"OK then, Malcolm. If you *are* Malcolm. You've lived with us for five years. If you like animals so much – if you care about your pets like a normal lovely owner…"

"Yes?" gasped Malcolm.

"Which one of us is Ticky and which one is Tacky?"

There was a long pause. Every animal in that garden – and there were quite a lot of them now – looked at Malcolm. Malcolm looked at the cats, the brown one and the white one. He knew this. He surely knew this.

"Come on, Malc…" said Zsa-Zsa.

"Yes, you can do it, Malcolm," said Mabel.

"We've got faith in you!" said a Dolly.

"Faith!"

"We believe in you!"

"Please, Malcolm," said Bjornita. "Don't let us down."

Malcolm stared again at the cats. They were wearing collars. But he couldn't see the writing on them. And at some level, he didn't want to cheat.

Eventually, he said – his voice now a total whisper:

"You – the white one – Tacky. You – the brown one – Ticky."

There was another long pause. And then the white one put its front paw up, and turned its collar, so that the coin of the collar was resting on top of its paw. "What does that say?" said the cat.

Malcolm could have lied but he didn't.

"Ticky," he said.

There was one more long pause, and then all the Orwell Farm animals silently turned, and left the front garden.

CHAPTER FORTY-THREE

He's Argentinian

The last thing Malcolm saw before he started to lose consciousness, though, wasn't his animal friends leaving sadly and shaking their heads. Nor was it Ticky and Tacky (having lost interest in the pigeon, now that they realised it wasn't a pigeon) going back through the cat flap.

Nor even his mother stepping out into the garden, not noticing him and starting the car.

Nor the streetlights softly coming on.

He saw all those things, but they weren't the *last* thing he saw. The last thing he saw – as his tiny damaged head wheeled round back towards his own house, that he used to live in, so safe and sound – was his own bedroom, on the first floor.

From the ground, he could see up into it. He saw a light come on in there, and with his still-strong bird vision, he saw, in the corner of his room, a cage that had been put there, on top of a table near the window. Inside, a small furry creature with enormous ears was running around. A memory came back to him, a word he had learned in school, in the time before, the time when he was a boy: *nocturnal*.

Which gave him, even in his terrible state, an idea. He fought against the oncoming tide of blackness, the soft rush of sleep, and flapped his damaged wings. With a supreme effort, and with a lot of pain, his broken body lifted.

Slowly, tremblingly, Malcolm rose, towards the

window of his bedroom. He hovered there for a second, looking in. He was right: inside, Chinny the Chinchilla was up, running around the room, the door of his cage having been left open to expend all his pent-up night-time energy.

Malcolm watched Chinny running around his floor, under his bookshelf full of books about computers and football and soldiers and all the other things boys like – because that's who Malcolm Bailey really was: a boy.

With the last ounce of strength he had left, Malcolm flapped his wings and threw himself against the glass. It only made a very small bang. But it was enough to make Chinny look over. The chinchilla jumped up immediately and sat looking quizzically on the other side of the window.

"Chinny!" whispered Malcolm, his voice cracked. "Chinny! Can you hear me?"

"*Que?*" said Chinny. "*No estoy seguro de lo que está diciendo el señor de la paloma...?*"

Oh, for crying out loud, thought Malcolm, through the pain. *Of course. He's* Argentinian.

But: this close to his boyhood self, looking at his own posters and toys, he found that the memory was there, of bits and pieces of Spanish that he had learned at school.

"Chinny... Chinny. Listen. *Soy... Malcolm.*"

"*Señor Malcolm? El niño? Que vive aqui?*"

"If that means 'the boy who lives here', yes... I mean, *si...* not another Malcolm..."

"*Por qué eres una paloma?*"

"It doesn't matter why I'm a pigeon. I just am. But look. Firstly, I'm sorry. *Lo siento...*"

"*Por qué?*" said Chinny.

"For not being nice to you when mum and dad gave me you as a birthday present. For not accepting you. I don't know how to say any of that in Spanish.

I hope you understand."

Chinny looked at him. Then, slowly, nodded.

"And secondly, I'm going to go to sleep now." Malcolm's exhausted mind struggled for the word. "*Dormiré*. But you have to stay there. While I go to sleep. Don't go away. No... *vaya*. Can you do... that for me... please?" Malcolm's tiny watchful pigeon eyes finally shut. But just before he actually lost consciousness he remembered one last bit of the chinchilla's language.

"*Por favor*," he whispered.

CHAPTER FORTY-FOUR

Begins with M

"Hello, Mr Barrington!" said Jackie.

"Oh, hello, Mrs Stone!" said Mr Barrington.

"Er... no, Mrs Stone is Fred and Ellie's mum. That's her over there," said Jackie.

"Where?"

"Over there. With... the large – the well-proportioned – the bigger-than-average – you know – husband."

"Oh yes. Very good."

To be fair to Mr Barrington, it was quite hard to see who was who. The bus had only just stopped outside the school gates – with a huge creak of the handbrake – and every child in Year Six had piled out at once. Now all the parents were trying to pick up their child at the same time. And it was getting dark.

"Um…" said Jackie, "where's Malcolm?"

"Malcolm! Yes!" said Mr Barrington, looking around. "He's… where is he…? Ah, here!"

"Hello!"

"Er… hello, Morris," said Jackie.

"I beg your pardon?" said Mr Barrington.

"That's Morris. Morris Fawcett."

"Oh," said Mr Barrington, looking at Morris. "Wait a minute. Didn't I give you my phone? When…" He turned away from Morris, to Jackie, "…*you* called. To speak to your son? A couple of days ago?"

"You said that was my mum," said Morris.

"Well. Yes. I did. But clearly it wasn't. Couldn't you tell?"

"Naah." Morris nodded towards Jackie, whose face had become very concerned. "She called me M…"

"Right. Is that what your mum calls you as well?" said Mr Barrington.

"No. But…" And here Morris frowned, as if a great and long thought was involved in what he was going to say next, "…she *might* do. Because my name. It begins…" His eyes went down and his lips moved, as if spelling it out in his head: then he looked up again, "…with M. Innit?"

Morris smiled, pleased with himself. For a second, Mr Barrington smiled too, pleased that Morris had understood *something*.

But it was literally for a second, before he went white with fear, on hearing Jackie scream:

"Mr Barrington!! Where is MALCOLM!?"

CHAPTER FORTY-FIVE

Free cheese

"No!" said Jackie, tearfully, driving back and speaking on her (hands-free) phone. "They *don't* know!"

"Well, how can that be?" said Stewart.

"I don't know!"

"Well, look, darling, I've called the farm."

"And?"

"And, er... well, they don't know where he is either..."

"Oh! Oh!" said Jackie.

"But: the very nice man there said they think he must just have missed the bus, because he went out playing in the fields or something and forgot the time. They're going to look for him now."

Jackie, by this time, had reached Kendal Road and was parking the car.

"He offered me some free cheese too," said Stewart. "Sounded quite nice."

"NEVER MIND FREE ********[56] CHEESE," said Jackie. "I think we should call the police!"

"No… darling. Let's just wait and see. They've said it's happened before, a kid missing the bus."

"Well…" said Jackie, slamming the car door and opening the front gate, "OK. But if they get back to us and say they *can't* find him, then I'm phoning

---

[56] Jackie used quite a big swear here, I'm afraid.

999 straight away, and – OOOOOOOHHH!!"

"What is it?"

"Come outside. Quickly!!"

CHAPTER FORTY-SIX

Very, very faintly

The whole family stood, silently, on the front garden path, looking up at Malcolm's bedroom window, where, as far as they could see, Chinny the Chinchilla was unconscious on a ledge.

"How did he get out?" said Stewart. "Do you think it was the cats?"

"Might have been," said Grandpa. "They might have dragged him out through the bars of his cage. Like in the war."

"Dad," said Stewart, "can you shut up about the war. You weren't even *alive* during it."

"Fair enough," said Grandpa.

"He wasn't in his cage," said Libby. "Last thing I saw he was running around the room…"

"Well," said Stewart, going into the house, "I'll go and get him off the window ledge…"

"This is terrible," said Jackie.

"Can I…?"

"No, Bert, you can't!" Jackie paused, and looked down. "It's terrible because… it's an *omen*," she said, saying the word 'omen' very ominously. "Don't you see? Chinny was Malcolm's pet. And now…" she began to cry, "Malcolm's gone missing!!"

"Jackie," said Grandpa, "we don't know if he's gone missing…"

"If the chinchilla's dead, then it might mean that Malcolm is… that Malcolm is—"

She was interrupted by the loud sound, from above, of Stewart's voice.

"Hold on a minute!" he shouted.

They all looked up. Stewart had opened the window, and was bending over the chinchilla.

"He's not dead. I can see him breathing. Very, very faintly."

The rest of the family, still standing in the front garden, took this in. Jackie nodded. Her face acquired a determined look.

"Right," she said. "Libby! Get a box!"

"Where are we going?" said Libby.

"To the vet's!"

"But it's Sunday!" said Stewart.

"I'm the receptionist. I've got the keys, and Rodney's home number. He owes me for working there for a pittance for twenty years!"

And with that, she headed back towards the car.

Once they were all *in* the car, and on the way to the vet's – with the unconscious chinchilla in a box on Bert's knees – the Bailey family were very focused. They were going to save the chinchilla.

It was probably good they were so focused, because that mission might have got confused – they might even have turned the car round, and stopped it – if they'd noticed, staring out of Malcolm's bedroom window, watching them leave, another, very similar-looking Andean Lanigera Chinchilla.

CHAPTER FORTY-SEVEN

Seventy-two hours

The Baileys had been sitting in the waiting room at Braden's Veterinary Surgery for nearly three hours. The clock on the wall said 10.45pm.

Jackie was resting on her husband's shoulder.

"I really think," whispered Stewart, "that you should go home."

"Who's you?" said Jackie, waking.

"All of you," he said, looking round. Grandpa and Libby and Bert were all there as well, sleeping on chairs, underneath pictures of cats and dogs and hamsters.

"I think they want to be here," she said.

Stewart looked to the door at the end of the room, the door where the surgery was.

"How long did Rodney say he thought it would take?"

Jackie shrugged. "He wasn't sure. The injuries are bad. And Chinny's a very small creature."

"I know."

"He said he would do his best."

"Yes," said Stewart. "And if there's one thing we know about Rodney, it's that he likes a chance to show off what a great vet he is…"

Jackie nodded. She took her phone out of her coat and peered at the screen. There were no messages on it. "Have you heard anything from the farm?" she said.

"Yes. I just got a text."

She sat up, turning to him. "And…?"

"They've called off the search. For tonight."

Jackie stood up, her teeth clenched. "Right. Time to call the police."

Stewart looked very worried. He glanced around, making sure the other members of the family were asleep.

"Jackie," he whispered. "I already *have* called the police."

Jackie went white. "You have? What did they say?"

"They said normally they don't put any kind of police search in place until someone has been missing for seventy-two hours."

"Three days!"

"Yes. They said a lot of boys of Malcolm's age run away for a bit, and then just turn up."

Jackie took a deep breath. She picked up her coat. "Let's go to the farm! I want to check myself!"

"No, darling…"

"Why not?"

"Because he might be making his way back

somehow. Hitch-hiking. Or on a bus or a train. And so it's better for us to be here for him – what if we find out he's made it to the city, but then we're miles away in the country...?"

Jackie shook her head, defeated. She folded her coat and sat back down next to her husband.

"They—" he said.

"The police?"

"Yes... they said to get back to them tomorrow if there was no news."

Jackie shut her eyes "I feel so awful, Stewart..."

"I know, darling," he replied.

"No, I don't just mean because I'm so worried. Also because... almost the last thing that happened with Malcolm before he went off on that trip was... us all laughing at him... because of the Monkey Moment..."

Stewart frowned. "Jackie," he said, "you mustn't..."

"I can't bear it. I can't bear that he's out there

somewhere and his last memory of us is that. Especially me. I'm his *mum*." Softly, she started to cry. "I shouldn't have laughed…"

"Jackie," said Stewart, putting his arm round her, and folding her crying face into his chest, "Malcolm's going to be OK. I know he is."

He said it very confidently. But his face didn't quite go with his words.

CHAPTER FORTY-EIGHT

Here we go

Next thing she knew, Jackie Bailey was having a dream. It was a dream in which there were lots of animals and lots of children, some of which were her children and some of which weren't, and the children and the animals kept on getting mixed up, and the children were chasing the animals, but then the animals were chasing the children, and all she could hear was quacking and mooing and barking and meowing and...

…then she woke up and realised that Bert was not sleeping any more. He had got hold of Stewart's phone and was pressing all the icons on AnimalSFX over and over again.

"Bert…" she said, sleepily, "can you stop that, please."

But before Bert did stop it, Rodney Braden came out of the surgery.

"Hello, Jackie," he said, quietly.

"Oh, Mr B," said Jackie. "Sorry, I must have fallen asleep. What time is it?"

Mr Braden looked up at the clock.

"Just turned five am."

"Oh, thank you so much for working this late. It's so good of you."

"It is good of me, yes."

"So…?" said Jackie, after an awkward pause. "How is he?"

As Jackie said this – slightly louder and more

insistently than perhaps she meant to – all the others began to stir.

"Well," said Rodney, smiling – his special 'what-a-great-vet-I-am' smile – "perhaps you all should come and see."

He took the Bailey family over to the surgery.

"OK. Here we go."

And he began to open the door.

CHAPTER FORTY-NINE
COCK-A-DOODLE-DOO

On the other side of the door, lying on a tiny operating table, the chinchilla's eyes began to open. This awakening wasn't quite like all the others in this story, though. He'd been under an anaesthetic, which had put him really fast asleep. So as he came round he was a little confused.

Images went through his mind. Of many different animals, and of many different places. But one thing kept coming back to him. It was quite hard for his waking mind to place it – but it seemed to be a goat. And the goat seemed to be saying something about how… about how he had to make sure that he ended up next to an animal he really loved, and who loved him. That this was how he would become what he was meant to be.

Then, suddenly, he heard a noise.

COCK-A-DOODLE-DOO!

And then again.

COCK-A-DOODLE-DOO!

The chinchilla felt frightened. He looked up. He seemed to be in an operating theatre… so why… was he hearing a cockerel?

Then he thought of something, with horror:

The third crow of the cockerel.

Time had run out. This was it. He was going to be – *forever* – whatever animal he saw next.

But then, even through his fear, something struck him. That crow didn't sound like any cockerel had sounded in the last few days. In the last few days, when he had been an animal, he had *understood* the crow; he knew the cockerel had actually been telling the other animals to wake up.

Cock-a-doodle-doo was just how *humans* heard it. Which must mean…

He looked round as the door opened. It all seemed to be happening in slow motion.

Then he heard a human voice – a woman's – say: "Bert! Can you stop doing that?"

"But I've never pressed that one before. The big chicken with the silly rubber glove on his head!"

"Yes, I know, Bert. But not now."

And then he saw that coming through the door *was* an animal he really liked; a *number* of animals he really liked; loved in fact; and who loved him.

Just as K-Pax had told him he had to find.

It was his family. Because humans, of course, *are* animals. We are just apes, who walk upright, wear clothes, and don't throw poo around quite as much.

"Now," said Rodney, blocking the family from coming in straight away, "I should warn you. This was a very complicated operation. It stretched me to the fullest. I had to use all my surgical talents…"

"Yes, we get that," said Stewart, trying to squeeze past him. But Rodney wasn't having it.

"He'll make a full recovery, but he'll be groggy for a while. Might not seem quite like his old self, at least to begin with."

"No, we understand that," said Grandpa, also trying to get past him.

"I just want you to be prepared for every eventuality."

"We are prepared, Rodney!!" said Jackie, with some edge in her voice.

"OK," said Rodney, stepping out of the way quickly – sounding a tiny bit frightened of Jackie –

and letting them see the patient.

Who was lying quite uncomfortably now, on the tiny operating table. He was lying quite uncomfortably because he was suddenly much too big for it.

And it was true, the chinchilla did not look at all like his old self. Or rather, in a way, he did: he looked like who he actually was and always had been; an eleven-year-old boy, called Malcolm Bailey.

Everyone – including Rodney – looked astonished.

"Hello, Mum. Hello, Dad," said Malcolm, weakly.

"Well," said Rodney. "Even I wasn't prepared for *that* eventuality."

CHAPTER FIFTY

Where's the chinchilla?

After everyone had finished hugging Malcolm –
and after everyone[57] had finished kissing him –
Stewart said:

"What are you doing *here?* What happened?"

Malcolm thought for a moment. Then he
said:

"I *was* on the school bus, Mum. When you came

---

[57] Everyone, not including Mr Braden.

to pick me up."

"What?" said Jackie.

"Yes! But I was hiding. I stayed on, behind one of the seats at the back."

"Why?"

"For a joke. But it went on a bit too long, and I didn't realise you'd gone away. And then when I came out, *everyone* had gone."

"Oh!"

"So then I came home. I walked from school. But when I got back, you weren't there. And I didn't have a key."

"Oh, yes, Jackie, we rushed here, didn't we! With Chinny! Of course!"

"So I walked around for ages looking for you. And then eventually I saw our car here, parked round the back. So I came in through the rear door, and found myself in this room. And Chinny was on the table."

"Malcolm!" said Jackie. "You shouldn't have done that! Stayed on the bus, I mean! I was calling you and calling you…!"

"Yes. I'm really sorry…" he said. His mum shook her head, trying to stay cross. But then her face melted, and she rushed to hug him again.

"Oh well! As long as you're safe and sound," she said.

"Um…" said Rodney. "Where's the chinchilla?"

From under the table, Malcolm picked up a red box. It was the box they'd used to bring Chinny to the vet's yesterday evening.

"He's in here," said Malcolm. "I put him in."

"Right. Can I have a look at him?"

"No," said Malcolm, swerving the box away from him. "I want to take him straight home."

"Really, Malcolm," said the vet. "I should check how he's doing."

"He's *fine*."

"Well, actually, he *is* fine. I know he's fine. Remarkably fine, actually. And I was rather hoping to reveal that to your family. In a kind of dramatic way, by opening the door and showing them their newly healthy chinchilla. I was looking forward to it. Well, you've stolen my thunder now. But still, I'd like to just—"

"*I want to take him straight home*," said Malcolm, intensely. "He's had a terrible experience and he needs to be back in his cage." Malcolm turned to his mum and dad. "Cos he's my pet and I love him!"

"You do?" said Jackie.

"Do you?" said Stewart.

"Yes," said Malcolm.

Jackie and Stewart turned to each other. Tears were in their eyes.

"Please, Rodney," said Jackie. "I'll bring the

chinchilla in first thing tomorrow for you to have a look at. But please let Malcolm take him home now."

Rodney looked a bit unhappy, but nodded.

CHAPTER FIFTY-ONE

Not normal circumstances

When they got home, Malcolm went straight up to his room. He opened the door, and rushed over to the chinchilla cage. He took off the top of the box, opened the door of the cage, and then shut it again. And then turned round to see his family coming into his room.

"Oh!" said his mum. "Chinny looks amazing!"

"He looks so well!" said his dad. "Like he'd never even left his room!"

"Yes! Exactly like he did before!"

"Mr Braden is clearly an amazing vet," said Malcolm.

"Yes!" said Jackie.

"He could probably operate on people."

"Well, I don't know about that," said Stewart.

"I do," said Malcolm.

Stewart frowned, but then Jackie said: "OK, everyone. It's been a very tiring day. And night." She checked her watch. "Five-thirty am. Time, definitely for bed."

Ten minutes later, after he'd brushed his teeth and put his pyjamas on, Malcolm looked up at his parents from his bed. They looked back at him, their faces full of love and relief. In the corner of his bedroom, Chinny was running on his wheel.

"Will that stop you getting to sleep?" said Stewart. "We can take the wheel out if so."

"No," said Malcolm. "I like the sound of it."

"So…" said Jackie, "we haven't even asked. Did you have a nice time on the farm?"

Malcolm closed his eyes. "Yes. I did. I really did. Thanks so much for sending me."

"And…" said Stewart, carefully, "that thing you said at the vet's. Is that true?"

"Which bit?" said Malcolm.

"About the chinchilla. When you said, 'he's my pet and I love him…'"

Malcolm opened his eyes again. He was glad that had been his dad's answer.

Because *not* everything he had said at the vet's had been true. When he'd woken up from the anaesthetic, and discovered he was a boy again – which was only two seconds before his family had come in and seen him on the operating table – Malcolm had had to think very quickly.

He had thought very quickly, and decided, very quickly, to make up the thing about staying on

the bus – and pretend that he had put Chinny into the box. Because Chinny wasn't there – had never been there. Chinny had been looking out of Malcolm's bedroom window the whole time.

Malcolm wasn't a boy given to making things up. But in this particular case, he'd decided there was no point in trying to tell his family what had actually happened. They just wouldn't believe him. No one, he knew, would ever believe him.

He knew he shouldn't lie, under normal circumstances. But these were not normal circumstances.

And: one part of it had not been a lie. The last, and most important part: the part that his dad was asking him about now. It would've been a lie only three days ago, but now he could feel how true it was.

"No, Dad. I do really love Chinny." And just to reiterate that, he turned to the tiny creature, who'd stopped running for a second on his little wheel, and said: *"Te amo, Chinny."* At which point, Chinny seemed almost to nod… almost to smile… and then just started running as fast as he could, making that wheel spin for dear life. "In fact," said Malcolm, "I love all animals!!"

Stewart and Jackie turned to each other, with tears in their eyes again, but smiles on their faces too.

"TATUFTB," said a voice in the doorway. Everyone looked round.

It was Grandpa.

"What does that mean?" said Libby, poking her head round the door, with a toothbrush in her mouth.

"That's a turn-up for the books," said Grandpa.

FIRST CODA:

One week later

Next Sunday morning, Malcolm insisted that they get to the zoo as early as possible. As well as, obviously, insisting on coming himself, for the first time for years.

They were the first people through the gates. Malcolm said "Hello!" to Sanjit and Luke, who looked confused, because he said it as if he'd met them before.

Then when they were in the zoo proper, Stewart

said: "So! Where would you like to go first, Malcolm? Lions? Tigers? Reptile House? Insect House?"

"I'd like to go to the petting zoo, please."

Stewart looked surprised – the petting zoo: wasn't that a bit babyish? – but said: "OK!"

Stewart was even more surprised that, after they got there, Malcolm wanted to stay at the petting zoo for so long. But he did seem really happy, being able to stand right inside the pen and stroke all the animals in there.

Then Stewart checked his watch, and said: "Listen, Malc— Oh, sorry, Malcolm…"

"Malc is fine, Dad."

"Is it?" said Jackie.

"Yes, Mum."

"Well, anyway," said his dad, "we want to go and see the… well, the chimps. I know you might not want to do that after the… the Monkey… you know…"

"Chimps are apes, not monkeys, Dad."

"Are they?"

"Yes. And I'll join you there in a bit."

"Oh. OK. You sure?"

"Yep. Just make sure you – especially Bert – stand back a bit from the bars…"

Stewart nodded. "Right you are," he said.

And they went. Malcolm watched them go. Then he looked around. No one else was in the petting zoo. Well. No other *humans*.

So even though there were a lot of other animals in there – and he wasn't entirely sure if his ones were the ones he thought they were – Malcolm said:

"Ludwig. Mabel. Zsa-Zsa. Trotsky. Benny. Bjornita. Snowflake. Dolly. Dolly. Dolly. Listen. I can't remember if all of you understand human, but I just wanted to say… firstly, I've told the keepers here where you're from. They didn't believe me at first, but then they rang the farm to check, and would you believe it, a cat, a dog, two pigs, a white horse, three sheep and a pair of tortoises were missing – so you'll all soon be going back to Orwell Farm. Where I think you'll be happier. And secondly, I just wanted to say… thank you. For bringing me back to my family. For saving me from my own cats. And just for teaching me how amazing animals are."

Malcolm looked up. None of the animals seemed to be doing anything, or reacting. He felt a little sad about this. Maybe they didn't understand human after all.

Or… maybe the whole thing *hadn't* actually happened. Maybe he'd fallen asleep in front of the goat pen – or maybe even just on the bus back – and dreamt it all.

"Anyway," he said, turning to go. "I love you all. I really love you all."

As he said this, a cat, a dog, two pigs, a white horse, three sheep and a pair of tortoises emerged from all the other animals, and surrounded him, rubbing and stroking themselves against him.

Malcolm smiled, he really really smiled, as the cat purred, the dog wagged its tail, the pigs grunted happily, the horse neighed, and the sheep baa-ed.

Oh, and the tortoises made weird squeaky noises.

From quite far away.

SECOND CODA:

One year later

"What are you doing in there?" said Mr Barrington. "Come on, it's time for bed!"

Mr Barrington was concerned. Last year on this trip to Orwell Farm a pupil had gone missing – for a small amount of time – and he held himself responsible. He was absolutely insistent that this wasn't going to happen again. So, this time, every night of the week, he'd stayed up to check that all of Year Six had gone into the farmhouse at the end of the day.

Then, after checking the rooms, he'd walked through all the barns and all the animal pens to make sure there were no children not safely in bed. He had felt terrible about that boy – Matthew, was it? Michael? – who had disappeared briefly before. Even if he had turned up safe and sound eventually.

And now – wouldn't you believe it? – there again appeared to be a boy not in his bed: in the goat pen, in fact. It was quite dark in there, and Mr Barrington was aware that his eyesight was not of the best. It had got worse since last year – *and* he was tired from doing this every night – but those eyes definitely seemed human. Didn't they?

Mr Barrington opened the pen gate and went in. *Hmm*, he thought, looking down – *bit muddy to go any further*. He squinted into the dark. Yes, those were definitely two eyes, looking at him. Quite large eyes, and he couldn't quite make out the colour (brown?

amber?), but he felt sure it was a boy or girl. It couldn't possibly have been an animal looking at him that keenly. Those eyes knew who he was, there was no doubt about that.

"Come on now. I know you might think you've got into trouble for staying out, but we'll discuss that in the morning," said Mr Barrington.

By Mr Barrington's standards, that was fairly lenient talk. He even said it in what he thought was a gentle, friendly voice. But still, the eyes kept on staring at him.

"Look, I really don't want to have to come in there and get you," he said. Which he didn't. He could feel his nice patent leather shoes – the ones Mrs Barrington said really suited him – sinking into the mud.

He decided to try a different tack.

"Look. We all love the animals. We all want to spend more time with them. This may sound silly, but sometimes, at the end of the day, I look out on the farm, at the sheep and the cows and the horses grazing, and I think, how wonderful it would be to be like them. To be an animal, with no money worries, no books to mark, no difficult pupils to make behave –" Mr Barrington was warming to his theme now, and starting, himself, to believe it – "not a care, really, in the world. It must be a wonderful life. But the truth is…"

He was about to say that the truth was that, obviously, we *can't* become animals, just because it looks nice, and because, as humans, we'll always be curious about how they think. We have to buckle up and get on with our own lives, and right now, that means coming out of the dark and going with me back to the farmhouse!

He was about to say that, very clearly, and he was sure that his speech would bring whoever was hiding in the goat pen out, and then everyone would be accounted for.

What happened instead was that he felt very… very… sleepy. It was late, and he was, as we know, tired. And somehow, while looking at those deep, amber eyes – the ones that seemed to know who he was, and belong to someone who was, clearly, listening and understanding him – that tiredness increased.

So he said:

"...obviously, we can't... be... com... annii... we... no..."

And that was as far as Mr Barrington got before he fell asleep, face down in the mud.

There was a pause of about ten seconds while the amber eyes watched and blinked. And then K-Pax came out of the dark, sniffed at the head of the strange human – already changing into something furry – and went back into the dark.

Acknowledgments

Thanks must go as ever to my fantastic team at HarperCollins Children's Books, principally the amazing Nick Lake, the tireless Paul Black and Geraldine Stroud, and the commander-in-chief Ann-Janine Murtagh; and thanks also to Kate Clarke, Elorine Grant, Samantha Swinnerton, Brigid Nelson, JP Hunting and Nicola Way; as well as Julien Matthews and Grace Rodgers at Avalon.

I'd like also to thank my collaborator, the incredibly talented Jim Field, who makes these words come alive in pictures; my literary agent and invaluable margin-scribbler Georgia Garrett; audio-book whisperer Tanya Brennard-Roper; my assistant and general helpmeet, Stasia Kolasa; my children, Dolly and Ezra; and my soulmate, Morwenna Banks.

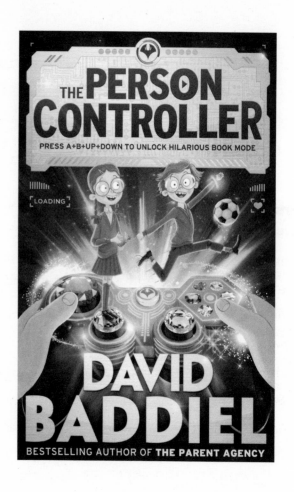

Don't miss David Baddiel's

THE PERSON CONTROLLER,

a thrilling, funny and touching adventure

from the new star of children's books –

out now in paperback.

Fred and Ellie are twins. But not identical (because that's impossible for a boy and a girl). They do like all the same things, though. Especially video games. Which they are very good at. They aren't that good, however, at much else – like, for example, football, or dealing with the school bullies.

Then, they meet the Mystery Man, who sends them a video-game controller, which doesn't look like any other controller they've ever seen. And it doesn't control any of their usual games. When the twins find out what it does control, though, it seems like the answer to all their problems. And the key to all their wildest dreams. At least it seems like that…

Turn the page for an extract…

CHAPTER 1
Fred and Ellie

Fred and Ellie Stone were twins. But they were never sure whether or not they could call themselves identical. They certainly shared exactly the same birthday (20th September, eleven years ago) and they had the same mum and dad (Eric and Janine). But their names were Fred and Ellie. And a boy and a girl are, clearly, not identical.[1]

Yet they *felt* identical. They sometimes even felt

---

[1] A boy and girl can only be fraternal twins, never identical. But don't ask me to explain the difference. It's a bit yucky.

that they knew what one another were thinking. And, even if they were 200 metres apart, they could mouth words at each other and always know what the other one was saying. They did look

pretty identical too. They both wore glasses and, most of the time, their school uniforms (even though uniform wasn't compulsory at their school). And they both, at the point at which this story begins, had braces on their top teeth.

They also both *liked* the same things. These included: superheroes; Japanese fantasy animation films; comics; maths (yes, they actually *liked* maths – sometimes they

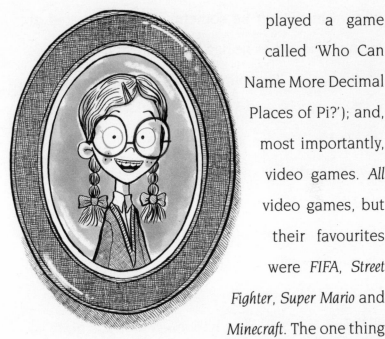

played a game called 'Who Can Name More Decimal Places of Pi?'); and, most importantly, video games. *All* video games, but their favourites were *FIFA*, *Street Fighter*, *Super Mario* and *Minecraft*. The one thing they would save up their not-very-much pocket money to buy was the most up-to-date versions of these games. Ellie, though, was better than Fred at video games.[2] Which Fred didn't mind. He knew she had quicker fingers and better hand-to-eye coordination.

---

[2] Fred was better than her at one thing, however: customising the avatars. He could customise any avatar on any game so the character on screen looked great – hairstyle, eye colour, skin colour, clothes, teeth, every shape and size. Fred sometimes wondered if he didn't like doing that even more than playing the games.

And, even though he sometimes got frustrated at losing, other times he just liked watching her fingers speed across her controller, as if she was playing a classical concerto by heart. And, when I say her controller, I mean *her* controller. Ellie and Fred always used their own ones. Ellie in particular was always very definite about which one was hers. The feel and the weight of her controller – even if, to the untrained eye/hand, both of them may have looked/felt exactly the same – suited her style perfectly.

Which was why what happened to it was quite so upsetting…

Find out what happens next in:

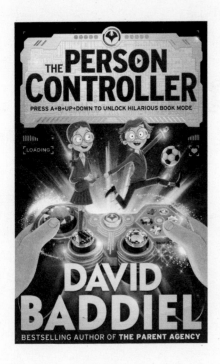

OUT NOW

Don't miss the award-winning debut novel from David Baddiel

Illustrated by Jim Field

"I wish I had better parents!" Barry said, a third time. And then suddenly the entire room started to shake...

Barry Bennett hates being called Barry. In fact it's number 2 on the list of things he blames his parents for, along with 1) 'being boring' and 3) 'always being tired'.

But there is a world, not far from this one, where parents don't *have* children. That's *far* too random for something so big and important. Instead, children are allowed to *choose* their parents.

For Barry Bennett, this world seems like a dream come true. Only things turn out to be not quite that simple...